NOWHERE MAN

SHEILA QUIGLEY

www.burgessworld.co.uk

First Published in 2012 by Burgess Books

British Library Cataloguing in Publication Data:
A catalogue record for this book is available from
the British Library.

ISBN-13: 9780956654649

Printed and bound in the UK by
TJ International Limited, Cornwall, PL28 8RW.

Burgess Books
Houghton-le-Spring
United Kingdom
www.burgessworld.co.uk

DEDICATION

For Leah, Jamie, Brenan, Harry and Siy

ACKNOWLEDGEMENTS

For booksellers everywhere, thank you.

ALSO BY SHEILA QUIGLEY

Run for Home
Bad Moon Rising
Living on a Prayer
Every Breath You Take
The Road to Hell
Thorn In My Side

To find out more visit:

www.theseahills.co.uk

1

NOWHERE MAN

PROLOGUE

Shelly Monroe opened her eyes. Slowly, she moved her head to the right and groaned loudly. What the----? she thought, feeling as if she'd been pushed through a meat grinder.

The memories came rushing back then, as her shaking fingers found the bandage around her neck. She pictured the raised knife coming towards her, and relived the horrendous pain as it bit into her skin and sliced across her neck. Amazed that she was still alive, and knowing that status could change at any moment, she muttered softly, 'Gotta get out of here, find some help. Like, now!'

She remembered how she'd suffered at the hands of his servants, how they had raped her repeatedly. She saw him leaning over her, smiling, his stinking breath in her face. As he slashed her throat, and how he had said sarcastically, 'Goodbye.'

Yeah, I'll goodbye you. Really I should be dead, but this dead bitch has been given another chance. A chance to wipe you scumbags off the earth.

'I know where you'll be!' she muttered, surprised she could talk at all. 'And I'm coming!'

Strands of her long black hair were trapped under her shoulder. She gagged at the memory of her hair being caught in the wound. A low moan escaped her as she relived the pain of her hair sliding through the slash in her neck, snagging on the stitches, to be slowly eased out, strand by sticky strand. Hair, like water, can get anywhere, she thought. Wincing in pain, her jaw clamped tight so as not to make a sound, she slowly, very gently eased her hair from underneath her neck and shoulder. She tried so hard not to scream, knowing they could be here now, watching her every move, catching her every breath. The thought made her shudder - but it also made her more determined than ever to seek justice.

This was the second morning she'd woken up not knowing where she was. She thought for a moment, then a chill swept through her. Only…only…this isn't proper morning! Her eyes flew to the window. Pitch black out there. Must be about two or three o'clock. So what the hell woke me up?

She sat up slowly. Apart from the soreness in her throat, she was feeling much better than she had the last time she'd been awake - except for the burning need inside for the drugs they had been feeding her for days in the monastery. She sighed, knowing she would have to overcome this need if the plans she was forming in her head were ever going to work.

Looking around the dimly-lit room, she shivered as a strange feeling of apprehension stole over her. She could see the guard through the window onto the corridor, a big meaty guy, but his presence gave her no comfort. Infact it made her want to laugh out loud - one man against the might of the Families!

A joke.

Even that Rambo copper Mike Yorke hasn't got the full picture. He'll be lucky if he lasts another day, if he keeps on storming about making waves all over the place.

He hasn't got a flaming clue what he's up against!

As if suddenly realising exactly what she herself was up against, her heart rebounded. She gave a small breathless sob of fear as she looked wildly around.

Got to get out of here, and fast.

For God's sake, I'm a sitting duck!

Knowing she had no time at all to waste, and beginning to feel the first surges of panic, she swung her feet over the side of the bed, ripping the tubes out of her arms. Blue hospital nightgown flapping open at the back, she placed one foot after the other onto the cold floor. Slowly she stood up, taking deep breaths, giving herself a small nod of encouragement as she felt no really bad side effects. Just a trifle weak.

'Oooh,' she moaned. Sore down there. The bastards, the dirty fucking bastards!

Must have been damn good stuff they've been pumping in to me here, though. Could have helped get rid of some of the shit. She'd been hooked up to quite a few different bags, dripping God knows what into her veins.

Giving the room another once over, she padded towards a cheap pale brown wardrobe beside the window. Opening the door, she heaved a sigh of relief. Her clothes, jeans, red t-shirt and black jacket were hanging there on old-fashioned wire coat hangers, black running shoes side by side on the floor. She reached to pick one of the hangers up and caught her finger on the uncovered hook.

'Now that's damned dangerous,' she muttered, shaking her hand and putting her finger in her mouth.

On the floor of the wardrobe, her black overnight case had toppled over and was lying on its side. Hopefully her insulin was also in there.

Thank you, God. She heaved a sigh of relief as she found her insulin pens. She needed her insulin more than anything. Clothes she could have nicked - a place as big as this had to have clothes lying around somewhere. Good that the clothes were here though, the last thing she needed was some crazy guard yelling his head off. Thank you Danny…or brothers!

Probably the Brothers Grim, she thought, kneeling down and rifling through the bag. Finding four more insulin pens in a side pocket, she smiled briefly. No way would Danny remember that stuff. She sat back on her heels and sighed at the thought of Danny.

Shit! Gotta get a move on. Right now, while most of the place is probably asleep.

Quickly she dressed, becoming more angry when she noticed

quite a lot of bruises on her body. No wonder I'm feeling stiff all over. The bastards!

Shuddering at the memory of where the bruises had come from and exactly what had been done to her, she paused for a second to brush the moisture from her eyes.

No point in feeling sorry for myself. I brought most of it on my own head, and now it's up to me to sort it.

Grabbing her bag, she moved quietly to the door. The police guard had his head turned to the left, as if he was watching someone walking down the corridor towards him.

Her heart sank at the sheer size of him. Shit! He's a big one all right. How the hell am I gonna get out of here?

Frustrated, she looked around. Damn. Nothing at all she could use as a weapon. Again she was flooded with self-doubt. Who am I to think I can take them on?

She sighed, and chewed her fingernail. If I had any sense, I'd give up now.

Yeah, well - to hell with that. Our Gary always says I've got no sense. He'll be pleased to know he's right for once.

Her heart rate speeding up more and more with the need to get away, thinking quickly and throwing caution to the wind she came up with a plan. Tearing her clothes off, she stuffed them into the bag, and put her nightdress back on.

She would say she needed to use the toilet, dress in the bathroom and climb out of the window. 'Yes, it might work… It's friggin' well gotta work… Got no other choice,' she muttered, making her way to the door again.

The guard was looking to the right now. If I can get this door open without making a sound, then run as fast as I can, I might be able to do it. After all, it's the last thing he's expecting.

As her hand touched the handle, she heard two quick thumping noises. A second later, the guard made a gurgling sound and fell to the floor.

She froze in horror.

Oh Christ!

It's them.

They've found me already!

The window.

Get out. Get out!

Who gives a shit if I'm just about buck naked.

Not me - and certainly not them!

Her heart going rapidly into overdrive, she reached the window in a few strides. Pushing it open, she looked down. Two floors. Damn. I'll break my legs.

What the hell am I gonna do?

Think! Think, for God's sake!

CHAPTER ONE

17 hours earlier

DI Mike Yorke ground out the cigarette with the heel of his shoe. He glanced over at Smiler, who quickly looked away.

Smiler, named for the up curving knife scars at each side of his mouth, could sense the anger coming from Mike. He could see it in his eyes, and was lost. Over the preceding three months, after years of mental and physical abuse, addiction to anything he could get his hands on, doing whatever it took to get it, no matter who got hurt in the process, Smiler had come to see Mike as his rock. He had at last found a home with Mike and his Aunt May, on the Holy Island of Lindisfarne just off the north east coast of England. He was finally living the family life he hadn't even known he was craving, for as long as he could remember.

But that life had been shaken to the core by the events of the last few days, leading to a night of pure horror. All Smiler could see ahead of them was more of the same- and a darkness so deep it was practically impenetrable.

'You'll have to go home,' Mike said suddenly, his voice low. He yawned and scratched the dark stubble on his chin.

Mike's silence over the last hour had worried Smiler as much as anything else. He knew that Mike was not by any means a quiet man. It had not taken him long to learn that if Mike was quiet, it usually meant trouble was brewing - and beware because he would be ready to explode at any time.

'What do you mean, home?' Trembling inside, Smiler waited for his answer, praying he didn't mean back down to London. That was the last place he wanted to be. He had finally come to know what home really meant. Home was Holy Island. Home was Mike. Home was Aunt May, now lying in a coma. Looking away, Smiler knuckled a tear out of his eye, and shoved his hands into the pockets of his dark grey tracksuit.

'To see to the mutt, of course, what else?' Mike said. 'He'll need walking and feeding, won't he? We already know he's the cleverest mutt ever born, but even he can't open a can of dog food.' Mike held his hands up and wiggled his thumbs. 'He ain't got any of these, see.'

'Clever shit,' Smiler retorted.

'Yup.'

Hiding his relief, and quickly looking the other way, while hastily drying his eyes with the sleeve of his jacket and praying Mike had not glimpsed his tears, Smiler sighed, before asking quietly, 'So where you going, like?'

'I've got things to do. Places to be.'

'What sort of things?'

'Smiler.' Mike waited until Smiler finally turned to look at him. 'You know what I have to do. You also know how dangerous it's gonna be. The last thing I want is you trailing after me and getting yourself into danger. There is so much yet for me to find out, and I don't want to drag you into harm's way.'

Smiler shook his head. His face turned ashen. 'No, Mike, don't go… I…I can't see any way back. Please, Mike, leave it. It's all black and I can't see anything past it.'

Mike sighed. He was bone weary, with the beginning of a nagging headache. 'I can't leave it, you have no idea what's at stake. And the little you do know puts you and the others at risk. So you leave it, eh?'

'No. I won't.' Smiler glared at Mike.

'You're gonna have to, Smiler. This is not a game. For God's sake, listen for once.'

'I can't… And you know what they say, a little knowledge is a bad thing. Just tell me all of it, so I can fucking well deal with it. All I know is that something bad is coming.'

'I suspect you know a lot more than you're letting on, anyhow. According to you, you and some of your friends know a hell of a lot, remember?'

Smiler scowled. 'But you don't believe me, do you? Even though I was right, more than friggin' once.'

'Sheer coincidence, mate.'

'So you keep saying, but you can't be sure of that.' Smiler shoved his hands deeper into his pockets, his mouth set in a stubborn line. 'Can you?'

Mike shook his head. 'Sorry, Smiler, but as far as I'm concerned, the least you know the safer you'll be. The safer you'll all be. And I need to know Aunt May will be looked after.'

'But Brother David----'

'Will really need your help. And be told when to sleep and when to flaming well eat, 'cause trust me, he'll sit there with his hands clasped together spouting a load of rubbish until he drops. Or the whole world collapses around him.'

Pushing his long lean frame off the wall he'd been leaning on, Mike looked up at the hospital. His dark eyes scoured the windows. He figured Aunt May's room was the fifth one along. As he stared at the window, memories came tumbling over each other as if blown by a reckless March wind.

Aunt May, strong and tall, demanding that she be allowed to foster three homeless boys. The only one standing in her way, her sour faced boss at Social Services, knowing he would never be able to replace her. He should have realised who he was taking on.

After a battle she refused to back down from, she won. They were to learn over their growing years that Aunt May never took on a fight she didn't win. Mike, Dave and Tony arrived on Holy Island two days later, three lost eight year olds wondering what was to become of them in this remote and beautiful place.

They need not have worried. Life with Aunt May on the island was good, very good. With her guidance, three boys teetering on the edge of society had grown into fine strong men. Two became detectives, one a monk.

We all owe her a debt we can never repay.

God knows how we would have turned out, if it hadn't been for her…all three of us!

Mike gritted his teeth as his eyes narrowed. But some bastard's gonna pay, that's a fact - one way or another. It's because of us. If we hadn't come to live with her on the island... If things had been different... If she'd left us in the kids' home, she wouldn't be lying in a coma now. He clenched his fist, picturing the pale face and frail limp body of this once strong woman, loved by all who knew her, lying helpless and unconscious in the hospital bed.

God help the bastards when I find them. Every single one of them, no matter how far I have to go. He punched the palm of his right hand with his left.

But now Mike was seriously worried. He couldn't get the idea out of his head that Tony was involved with a group of people who had been around forever, and made modern day terrorists look like a bunch of grannies on a Sunday School picnic. Worse, the idea that the whole world had been fooled for so long. It was practically unbelievable - or was it?

He looked at Smiler. 'You're a clever little shit, answer this.

How do we know the reports from the other side of the world are really what's happening?'

'Back off, man, you're losing the plot now.'

'OK, so - who's left alive to say the Romans really invaded us, or that Vikings once walked on Holy Island? Or that a man has really walked on the moon? The whole of history could be a fucking fairy story for all we know!'

'Doubt it.'

Mike shrugged. 'Prove it.'

'It's all written down.'

'Oh yeah?'

'All of it.' Sighing and shaking his head, Smiler got his cigarettes out. Mike held out his hand. Smiler frowned. 'You've just put one out.'

Mike shrugged. 'And?'

Pulling a face, Smiler handed a cigarette over.

'Cheers.' Mike lit the cigarette up, his thoughts now on what he had learned from Shelly about the intentions of the Families. It made his skin crawl every time he thought about it. Plus he had a feeling that she still hadn't told him the whole truth. No - he knew she hadn't told him everything. And he dreaded what else was to come.

He could feel Smiler's eyes on him as, taking out his phone, he tried Tony's number again.

He let it ring and ring. 'Where are you, bastard?' he said,

through gritted teeth, becoming more angry by the minute. 'Come on, get back to me, fucking prat.'

'He obviously doesn't want to talk to you.' Smiler said.

Mike tutted. He needed answers. It went against everything he believed in to even think that Tony could be involved with these monsters. But some of the things he knew pointed right at Tony's door. He continued to let the phone ring until Smiler nudged him.

Looking up, Mike watched as two police cars, followed by at least twenty other assorted family cars, began slowly pulling into the hospital parking lot, circling round and round like predatory wasps trying to find a vacant place. Smiler also watched them, then looked quizzically up at Mike.

'Gotta be the kids' parents,' Mike said, with a sinking feeling in the pit of his stomach. He nodded at Smiler. 'Glad their missing offspring have been found at last, I guess. Some of the poor sods will have been waiting for months. Hope they've come prepared for what they are going to find.'

Mike was proven right a few minutes later, as people got out of their cars and started a mass stampede towards the hospital entrance. There was another, much slower, group of about fifteen, dragging their feet as if trying to resist an invisible rope that was slowly pulling them towards the entrance. As Mike watched, a man and woman broke away from the main bunch and headed towards them.

'Some very happy faces and hearts there, then,' Mike said to the pair, managing to raise a smile for the first time in hours as he nodded in the direction of the running people.

'You must be DI Yorke? Sergeant Angela Rafferty,' the woman said in a gentle Irish voice. She held out her hand. 'Really pleased to meet you. I have heard so much about you from Jason, and now you're the local hero.' With her other hand, she flicked the long brown plait off her shoulder.

Holding onto her hand for a little longer than was really necessary, Mike said, 'Pleased to meet you too.'

Hmm, certainly a beauty this one all right, he thought, noticing the dimples when she smiled. Bet old Jase is enjoying his time guiding her around. Hope for his sake Samantha never meets her, or it'll be the third degree every night for the poor sod.

But a few fleeting seconds was all Mike would allow his attention to wander. Too much going on. He needed nothing to complicate things. He was back in police mode as soon as the man in front of him spoke.

'Hi, Mike.'

'Cox.'

Mike nodded at him. Detective Jason Cox, originally from Manchester, but now living and working in Newcastle in the same office as Mike. Extremely tall, in his middle forties and rapidly losing his pale ginger hair, he'd been around as long as Mike could remember.

He and Mike had always got along. It wasn't hard to get

along with Jason. Rather old fashioned in his thinking, and a bit of a fusspot, Jason Cox had surprised everyone - and himself - five years ago when, housebound with the flu, he had sat down with the computer he had always scorned, and found himself completely hooked. He practically became a computer whiz overnight. There was nothing he didn't know about them. Word had spread to the Met, and now he was begging off moving down to London. One reason was because he was quite happy where he was, and the other reason - which he made no bones about - was that his wife Samantha simply wouldn't allow it. In the Cox household, Samantha's word was law.

'Well done, Mike.' He slapped Mike's arm with a thick meaty hand, and grinned at him.

Mike nodded. 'Thanks, Jase. But It's not over yet - not by a long shot. I'm gonna need your help with some computer stuff. I'll let you know later. Ohh, and sorry, but where the hell did you dig that excruciating tie up from?'

Before Detective Cox could defend his choice in ties, Sergeant Rafferty inserted herself between them and said, 'Yes, Detective Yorke, there's some forty parents come to claim their kids. Sadly, another fifteen or so have come to claim their bodies. I'm told you are responsible for cracking the case?' she asked, one eyebrow slightly raised in a question.

Oh God, Mike thought. Shades of The Bill. Where the hell is she from?

'Yes.' He nodded, noticing the tension between her and Cox, guessing Cox, although a good man, must have somehow rubbed her up the wrong way. How? That was anyone's guess. Cox was usually a pussy cat with no claws. Although perhaps it's her and she's just a miserable git!

'No false modesty there, then, is there?' Rafferty smiled, flirting with her eyes.

'There never is,' Smiler muttered, scowling at Mike.

'Didn't you have somewhere to go, sunshine?' Mike replied, still looking at Sergeant Rafferty.

'Yeah, I do,' Smiler scowled, 'but I'm going up to see Aunt May now, OK? If that's all right with you, like. Brother David might have finally stopped his fucking useless praying. I'll be ready when you've sorted a fucking lift out---- What?' Mike was frowning at him.

Getting no answer, Smiler went on, 'You expect me to walk from Newcastle to Holy Island? No fucking way, man, you do it! ' He stormed off, leaving the question hanging.

'Hey,' Cox shouted. 'Who do you think you're talking to? Get yourself back here, young man.'

'You can fuck off an'all,' Smiler shouted over his shoulder.

'Come back here!'

'Just leave it,' Mike said, putting up a placating hand.

'Some edge he's got on him for a young kid, hasn't he? How old is he, anyhow? The cheeky little thing only looks about twelve or thirteen, for God's sake.' Sergeant Rafferty's top lip twisted in a snarl. 'If there's one thing I can't stand, it's a cheeky brat.' She watched Smiler, who had completely ignored Cox, make his way through the parked cars.

'Forget it,' Mike said.

Rafferty took no notice, and went on, 'And what's happened to his face? Those scars look like someone deliberately carved a smile on it.'

'Actually, he's nearly seventeen - and yes, he has an edge and the smile to go with it, as well as a reason for it. If you'll excuse me.'

'Oh. Sorry. Didn't mean to offend.'

'You haven't.'

But Sergeant Rafferty knew she had. The warmth she'd felt at first had quickly evaporated. Wondering what the story was with them, she watched as Mike followed Smiler into the hospital. Then, her eyebrows raised, she turned to look at Cox.

He shrugged. 'Never met the kid before. He's probably one of Mike's many waifs and strays. He collects them like other people collect autographs.'

Before Cox could say any more, a large thickset old man with a walking stick stopped in front of them. Leaning with both hands on his stick and staring at Cox, he said, with a Polish accent, 'My Annya - she...she is not there. Not with the living group… She is not with the other poor ones, either.'

'Sorry?' Sergeant Rafferty said, with a frown.

The old man swung his head towards her and said, 'My Annya - she is not there. Not with either of the groups.'

Cox stepped between them. 'I'll deal with this, Sergeant. I'm so sorry, Mr Brodzinski. I was led to believe that your granddaughter was one of the first group.'

The old man shook his head. 'No.'

Cox put a steadying hand on the old man's shoulder. 'Why don't you go home, Mr Brodzinski. Brod. I'll pop round sometime tomorrow, when we've had time to question a few of the more healthy ones we have. Get a bigger picture of what exactly has been going on with the kids.'

Mr Brodzinski sighed. Knowing there was nothing that he could do, he quietly said, 'OK,' as he hobbled off.

'What's the story with him, then?' Sergeant Rafferty asked, watching the old man.

'Well, for your information, Mr Brodzinski and his seventeen year old granddaughter Annya have been in the UK for more than two years now. He goes to my chess club. Damn good player he is, too, beat me more than once.'

'Oh, please. Chess club?' Sarcasm dripped from her words. 'More drains on our taxes.'

Ignoring her dig at his game, which he loved, Cox said, 'Actually Brod has his own money and, from what I hear, plenty of it. So, no- he's far from a drain on anything.'

Without waiting for her to answer, he turned and headed towards the hospital,hoping to catch up with Mike.

Tutting, and glaring at his retreating back. Sergeant Rafferty had no other option than to follow.

CHAPTER TWO

When Mike reached Aunt May's room, he paused a moment and looked through the open door. Smiler was sitting on the left side of the bed, holding Aunt May's hand, which, Mike thought, doing a neat double take, is a miracle in itself. I guess Smiler hasn't held too many hands in his life, poor sod.

And there was Dave. He could never bring himself to call him Brother David. Mike had kicked up a major fuss when Dave had said he was going to join the order on the mainland, and it had taken him quite a while to accept the fact of it. In truth, he never really had, and strongly doubted if he ever would. As far as Mike was concerned, Dave was wasting his life.

Why lock yourself away in a monastery? The whole idea of why someone would want to do that had puzzled Mike ever since Dave had told them that he wanted to join the brotherhood.

But most of the time he put on a good face, for Dave's sake. Although not brothers by birth they were, through Aunt May, much more than that. They shared a bond - and Aunt May was the glue that held them together. He stared at Dave now, and sighed without even realising.

Brother David's head was down and he was holding Aunt May's other hand. His lips were moving silently.

Ah, for fuck's sake, Mike thought, Smiler's right. He's praying again! Hours he's been at it now. When is he ever gonna learn? All them hours he prayed for help when he was a kid got him fuck all, and it ain't gonna get him anywhere now.

Silently Mike entered the room and stood at the bottom of the bed, his feet apart and his hands clasped behind his back, staring at Aunt May.

Smiler looked up at him and attempted a brief smile, which, knowing him, Mike interpreted as 'I'm sorry'. Giving him a wink to assure him that everything was fine, Mike gave an exaggerated cough to get Brother David's attention.

A few seconds later, Brother David looked up. 'You're back from wherever, I see.'

Well, if that isn't stating the obvious, as usual, Mike thought, pulling a face at him before saying, 'Yes, oh wise one, it's truly me standing before you. Although in truth, I haven't really been anywhere yet… Any change?'

Brother David slowly shook his head. 'The doctor came in a few minutes ago. He said some of the tests still aren't back yet. It might be a few days. He also said…' Brother David hesitated, before swallowing hard and looking Mike in the eye. 'He also said there might be some... some form of brain damage. But they're not sure, they only think she might,' he hurried on, seeing Mike's face. 'But you don't know, Mike, she could snap out of it tomorrow. Just wake up as if nothing's happened.'

'Bastards!' Mike gripped the metal frame at the end of the bed, his knuckles gleaming white. Turning quickly, he started pacing back and forth. Silently, Smiler and Brother David kept pace with their eyes. Suddenly stopping mid stride, Mike turned to Brother David. His eyes hard and staring, he snarled, 'Surely they must have some idea when she's gonna wake up, for fuck's sake? What are they in this place, friggin' amateurs?'

Brother David dropped his eyes and shrugged. He had been expecting this outburst. Mike had always been the most emotional of the three of them, and he'd never mastered the art of not to showing his emotions. 'A day, a week, a month, longer.' He shrugged again. 'Sorry, Mike, they don't really know.'

'Do they know any fucking thing?' Angrily, Mike started punching his hand as he went back to his pacing.

Smiler quickly swung his head from one to the other. Unable to help himself, he started to sob.

At once, Mike was at his side, his own feelings pushed away. Thinking only of Smiler, he said, 'The doctor only said might be, Smiler, and the docs always give you worst case. Isn't that right, Dave?' He rested his hand on Smiler's shoulder, giving it a gentle squeeze, expecting it to be repelled at any moment - Smiler allowed minimum physical contact - and willing Dave to agree with him about the doctors, for the kid's sake.

Smiler looked up at Brother David who, after a brief moment, silently nodded at him.

'Tell you what, would you rather stay here in the hospital? Maybe go home tonight, Smiler, at least for a proper night's sleep? Dave will call you if there's any change.' He looked at Brother David, who nodded again.

'Of course I will, Smiler.'

'Right. Sorted. I'll go and see Jill about Tiny, I'm sure she'll be all right about it until you get back tonight,' Mike said.

Sighing, Smiler replied softly, 'No. I want to stay here tonight as well, I want…I'm gonna stay here until she wakes up.'

Mike removed his hand from Smiler's shoulder, amazed that he hadn't shrugged it off after a few moments. Perhaps he's starting to trust me more, Mike thought, with a pleased sigh. Now that would be real progress.

'OK, we'll see how it goes. I've got some things to sort, before I leave. I'll go back to the island, see if Jill really will look after Tiny. If not, I guess he'll be all right in the dog pound for a day or two.' He pulled his mobile out and flashed it at Brother David, as if the brother had no connection to the present and didn't know what a mobile phone was. 'Do you remember the number, Dave?'

'I've got it,' Smiler put in, before Brother David, refusing to take the bait, smiled and nodded.

'There's one more thing I have to do before I go.' Mike pulled a small white envelope out of his pocket and moved closer to Aunt May, tipping the contents into his hand. Brother David's face lit up as he saw Aunt May's gold cross slide out of the envelope.

'Help me slip this under her neck, Dave.'

'I wondered where that was. She's never taken it off for... how many years?' Brother David smiled as he gently put his fingers under her neck, and caught the chain that Mike was pushing through from the other side. Catching it, he stretched across and put the chain into Mike's hand.

'Kristina found it when we went to examine the place she was attacked by them cowardly bastards. They must have ripped it off her neck just for the fun of it, or just because they could. I popped out first thing this morning and bought a new chain. Hopefully she won't notice when she wakes up.'

'Wouldn't bank on that one,' Brother David replied with a smile. 'We've never yet been able to get one over on her in all this time, have we?'

Mike slowly shook his head in answer, he took one more lingering look at Aunt May, and fastened the catch. He set the cross gently on her chest, kissed his middle and forefingers and placed the kiss on her cheek.

'You hurry up and get better, Aunt May. I'll always be thinking of you wherever I am, but there's something I've gotta do. I promise I'll be right back to see you as soon as you wake up. Nothing or no one will keep me away.' Then, without a backward glance at either Smiler or Brother David, he turned and walked out the door.

But neither of them had missed the tightening of Mike's jaw, nor the narrowing of his eyes.

'Mike's a doer, Smiler,' Brother David said solemnly.

'I know,' Smiler mumbled.

'Would you like to hold my hand in prayer?' Brother David reached his hand across the bed.

Smiler visibly shrank in on himself. Quickly, he put his head down and stared at his feet - but not quickly enough for Brother David to miss the look of horror on his face, leaving the monk wondering just what had happened to this child in his short life. Withdrawing his hand, he began to pray as tears ran down Smiler's face.

CHAPTER THREE

Kirill Tarasov paced the length of his oak paneled study, a glass of English vodka in his hand, a cigar in the other. Not his first choice in vodka, but that stupid brain-dead housekeeper had forgotten to restock, and not for the first time.

'Should have broken more than her jaw,' he muttered, staring out of the window at the Siberian winter. 'She's only alive because she's the best cook I've ever had, never thought I'd ever say it but ugly shrimp of a peasant is practically irreplaceable.' He turned to the other occupant of the room and shrugged. 'So what's wrong with you? They're only fucking peasants, for fuck's sake. It's not that when you're using them to chase away the nightmares after your morphine fix, is it?'

Before his son Vadim could answer, his oldest daughter, Lovilla, entered the room holding the phone. Lovilla was tall, blonde and slim, with a natural dark brown beauty spot at the corner of her mouth, of the type once so beloved of '50s American stars. 'Father,' she said before going on sarcastically with a sneer, ' the esteemed Earl Simmonds is on the video link. He says it's urgent.'

Vadim sniggered.

'Damn the man.' Tarasov put his drink on the table and, frowning at his son, wished as for God knows how many times before that a certain one of his illegal sons was the one standing in front of him, and not this pathetic legal. He moved over to the phone and took it out of Lovilla's outstretched hand.

'OK, Simmonds, it's only a couple of days since I saw you last. What the hell's so urgent it couldn't wait until next month?'

Quickly Simmonds gave him a brief run-down. When he was finished, he said, 'And so I'm calling a meeting for three days' time. Never have we been in such danger before. Even that, that bunch of flaming witches has never come this close.'

'Well, I do beg to differ there. Once or twice the bunch of flaming witches haven't been short of the mark. And, might I add, if your family had succeeded in wiping out the right ones in 1645, instead of burning and drowning ordinary peasants just to make a show, then we wouldn't have this trouble today. All that witch hunting only succeeded in driving the real culprits underground.'

'Why do you always insist on blaming my family for everything that ever goes wrong?' Simmonds snapped.

'Perhaps because they are.' Before Simmonds, who was practically foaming at the mouth, could let off more steam, Tarasov went on. 'But all of this ridiculous hoo-ha through one fucking man...Over-reacting a bit, as usual, aren't you? And what's going to happen in the next few days? Just allowing him to run free, are we, take the piss out of us?'

'No!' Simmonds was practically shouting now. 'As we speak, he is being dealt with.'

'Well, let's hope so. Also, when have we ever personally dealt with something as mundane as this ourselves? For God's sake, we are supposed to have people trained for this very thing who should be getting on with it. When did we ever dirty our hands? Really, it's all becoming very boring, to say the least.'

'For your information Tarasov, not one, but three top assassins have been assigned to him. I can't see him surviving much past the next twenty-four hours. In fact, there's a whole mop up going on, as well as extra people drafted in to look for that damn book.'

For a moment Tarasov was quiet. Lovilla frowned as she watched an emotion she rarely saw play across her father's face, before he said, 'So, if it's all in hand, why another trek so soon to your dismal part of the globe?'

Simmons bristled, giving the exact reaction Kirill aimed for. 'We all know the world can not go on as it is. Billions and billions of people increasing at such an alarming rate. And the world is warming far more rapidly than was predicted.'

Tarasov held up his hand. 'Oh please, spare me the details. It's all rubbish. As usual, you're panicking over nothing.'

'The meeting is in the usual place. Goodbye.'

Tarasov brought his palm down hard on the connection button, a disdainful snarl on his mouth. 'Fools, the lot of them.'

His son laughed again.

'I'm pleased you find it funny. The idiots are starting to believe the very myths that we started.'

Vadim shrugged.

'Can I come with you this trip, Father?' Lovilla hastily put in, before Vadim could say anything else to enrage their father. 'I would love to do some shopping in London. And I feel the need for the sun on my skin.'

'You are not long back from Spain.'

'And?' She pulled a face.

Tarasov looked at her as he thought it over, knowing full well that shopping was the last thing on Lovilla's mind. 'OK, why not. It's time a few of you were showing more interest in family matters.' He glared at his son, who shrugged, then cast his eyes over his sister. The look that passed between them was an undeclared act of war.

He watched as Lovilla, totally unconcerned about her brother and probably laughing to herself at the gauntlet he had just thrown down, left the room. Tarasov had always suspected that this daughter would be the one out of all of his legal children who would eventually take up the reins of the family empire. He was pleased, in a sense- she was the brightest, and the only one who delighted in the same culinary adventures as he did. And now he would have to watch her in case she became ambitious too soon.

'Huh.' Vadim stormed out. For a brief moment, the biting cold entered the room, as the door slammed behind him.

Tarasov moved to the window and watched his son storm along the veranda, knowing that he did not stand a chance against Lovilla. It was the way of the Families.

Still staring at the snow, he sighed as he pulled his mobile phone out and dialled a London number.

CHAPTER FOUR

Mike had hold of Tiny's lead. A few months earlier, when the world had been normal, and he'd first set eyes on this huge brute with the unlikeliest name, he'd called him the damned ugliest dog in creation. Now, though, he would be the first to admit that Tiny did have a certain charm, and that those large paws of his were wrapped firmly round Mike's heart. As soon as people got over their first impression, they learned to love him.

Mike stood at the water's edge on St Cuthbert's Isle, a little islet which, centuries ago, St Cuthbert had used for meditation. After a trial period of being a hermit, he moved to the more remote island of Inner Farne. Mike had been surprised when he found out that Smiler knew so much about the history of Lindisfarne, and of St Cuthbert.

But, he thought with a hint of a smile, seeing as St Cuthbert was credited with being a healer and a seer, Smiler's probably read the print off the page of every article he could find.

Tiny was enjoying himself as he ran quickly from side to side, picking up sticks, stones and any amount of rubbish and depositing it at Mike's feet.

Mike said good morning to a few locals as both they and their own dogs nervously eyed Tiny, frightened in case he wanted them for supper. They needn't have worried Tiny was gentle, loving and terrified of most animals a quarter his size.

Staring across the water at St Cuthbert's Cross, Mike thought about Aunt May. She loves it here, but will she ever see it again? Brain damage could mean anything, doesn't necessarily mean the actual brain. She could lose her legs or something, the use of an arm… Please let it be something like that. Anything other than actual brain damage.

Tiny came back with the latest offering, and dropped what looked like a child's grubby red and green striped sock at Mike's feet, and started nudging at Mike's hand.

Mike patted his head. 'Come on then, boy, we've gotta get you sorted out. I know you'll prefer the place I'm gonna see if they'll have you, rather than the police pound.'

Slipping his lead on, they walked through the village to their street- but instead of going into their own door, they moved one up. Mike entered Jill Patterson's back yard, and was just about to knock on the door when it opened.

'Hi, Mike.' Jill smiled at him. Mike was slightly taken aback- a smile from Jill was a very rare event.

'Hello… I, er... I need to ask you a favour, Jill.'

'Just ask.'

That fairly threw him. He had not known Jill very long, but the petite redhead was not usually so obliging. She had a reputation as a man hater, which had followed her from her previous job.

'Please, don't think you have to be obliged.'

'Well that depends what it is.' The smile grew wider and Mike would have sworn she was flirting with him.

She stepped away from the door and stood on the back of her slipper. As she bent over to put it back on her foot, Mike noticed how low her yellow top was, and was momentarily distracted from his tortured thoughts. Catching her green eyes as she straightened up, he expected at the very least a substantial tongue-lashing, but was pleasantly surprised when she smiled and motioned for him to come into the house.

'How can I help you, then?'

Jesus. She's been replaced by a flaming alien!

This is definitely not the Jill I know...

Before Mike could reply, the small kitchen was filled with squeals of delight as Jill's teenage daughters Jayne and Cassie came in and saw Tiny. Loving the attention, Tiny flopped down and rolled over, his massive paws waving in the air and his heavy tail thumping the floor, with a delighted girl at each side of him.

'Well, er, it's actually, it's about Tiny… I was wondering...'

'You need a dog sitter don't you?' Jill put in, her eyebrows raised in a question.

'I realise it's a bit of a cheek, and short notice. But he's no bother, and he'll be quite happy in the garden when you're out,' Mike said quickly, dreading her answer. Shit, I really shouldn't have asked her, she's under enough stress. I'll put him up in the police pound. He'll be all right there.

'Look, it's OK. It's a bit much to ask. And you're very busy. Wasn't thinking straight, sorry.' He turned to go.

'Mum!' Cassie squealed. 'He has to stay here. Please, Mum. We'll look after him. And better still, he'll look after us. Won't you, boy?' She patted Tiny's head, and was rewarded by a wet doggie kiss on her cheek.

'I'll walk him, promise, Mum,' Jayne said.

'Of course he can stay. We do have a much bigger garden than yours, and it's not exactly what you would call landscaped. It's the least I can do after----' Her eyes filled up, and she touched the top of Cassie's head. 'After what you did for us. You can leave him here until Aunt May gets out… She is?' The girls fell silent and looked quickly up at Mike.

Hesitating a moment, he said. 'Nothing's certain yet, still some more tests.'

'Oh, God,' Jill said, 'I'm so sorry. Of course we'll take good care of the dog. If there's anything else, anything at all, just let me know…Does she have her night clothes? In fact, I'll pop down later and pack for her - that's if you don't mind?'

'No, er, that's fine, thank you. Could you remind Smiler to take them in to the hospital tomorrow? Although,' he sighed, 'I'm not quite sure he'll be back tomorrow. Depends how things work out at the hospital. But she'll want her own stuff, I know that for a fact.'

Jill smiled. 'Of course she will, and will no doubt raise hell if she can't get them. We'll play it by ear. I don't mind taking her clothes in to the hospital.'

'Thanks, Jill, I really appreciate it.' Mike reached into his pocket and took out a note. 'Take this for the time being. He's a big eater, and a great lover of biscuits. Just let me know how much I owe you. OK, Smiler will be popping back and forth I'm sure… I...er…I have to go somewhere.'

She was silent for a moment, as if wondering where he suddenly had to go when Aunt May needed him, but said, 'Any special dog food he needs?'

'No, he'll eat anything.' He handed the twenty to Jill and started backing away from them. Turning at the gate, he gave them all a quick wave, then hurried along to Aunt May's cottage.

Quickly, he showered. Back downstairs, towel tied around his waist, he padded barefooted to the kitchen and made himself a ham and tomato sandwich, smothering it with mayonnaise. Sitting down at one of the small round breakfast tables that Aunt May used for her guests, he figured out his next step.

He would go in to Berwick. Strictly speaking, it wasn't his station any more, and he would be back working at Newcastle. The case was all but closed now, apart from some mopping up that he quite honestly couldn't ever see happening, not if what he knew was the solid truth. So he would also have to go to Newcastle, to report in and take leave that was owed to him. But he very much needed to talk to Kristina Clancy - hence the trip up to Berwick.

He finished the sandwich and quickly dressed in jeans and cream t-shirt. Rummaging in his overnight bag, he found a packet of cigarettes, which had been in there for months. Standing at the back door he lit one up as he looked over the fields towards the sea, knowing that it was a sight he might never see again.

Half an hour later he was on the road. The traffic was light, the sun was high, the sky was blue, but the only thing on his mind was Aunt May's grey face and the thoughts of what he would do to those scumbags when he found them.

And I will.

There were things missing out of the puzzle, but he had names. Another long talk with Shelly should clear a few things up, if the kid wasn't so friggin' muddled. Half the pieces of a puzzle were no good to any body, and sometimes got the wrong person killed. And in this instance, the killing wouldn't stop at just one.

Most of what she'd told him was pretty much unbelievable, until he had stopped and thought seriously about it. And that's all he had done for hours.

He didn't see the car come flying up behind him. He heard the sudden roar of the engine, though, and looked in his rear view mirror just in time to see the gun pointed at him. He ducked as the first bullet hit the back window, ploughed on through the car and shattered the windscreen just above where his head had been. As bullet after bullet rained down on the car, Mike grabbed the wheel tightly and started swinging the car from side to side, praying as hard as he could, at the same time pouring scorn on himself for doing so after the many times he'd scoffed at Brother David.

He was wondering, in a remote, terrified sort of way, just how close he was to the cliff edge. Although he couldn't see it without turning his head, the car was now riding abreast of him. On his third sharp swing to the left he smashed into its side, knocking the lighter car across the road, but sending his own car into a spin that brought him even closer to the edge. The other car must have righted itself, because suddenly another round of bullets hit Mike's car. This time, at least one of them found their mark.

CHAPTER FIVE

'Apple?' Brother David pulled a shiny red apple out of his pocket and handed it across the bed. Smiler was still for a moment, staring at the apple. Slowly, his eyes grew wider. He started to tremble, his stare shifting from the apple to Brother David.

'No, no…' He jumped up, knocking over the chair behind him.

Puzzled, Brother David stood up, as Smiler's trembling became a full-blown spasm and he started talking in double-quick time. Brother David hurried round the bed. Although Smiler was not focusing on him, it was as if he could see him coming anyway, as the boy backed away from him into the corner.

'Smiler? Smiler, what's wrong?'

As suddenly as Smiler had started, he stopped, and stared at Brother David. 'They're coming for him, they're coming for Mike on all sides. You've got to help him.' He grabbed the front of Brother David's robe and started to shake him. 'They're getting closer. He doesn't stand a chance, they're gonna kill him.' Sweat broke out on his brow and Smiler's whole body had started trembling again.

'Calm down, son.'

'You don't understand,' Smiler insisted. 'Mike's in trouble…big trouble.' He started to stamp his heels on the floor, as if he was having a fit.

Brother David decided the best course of action was to humour him. 'Do you know where he is, Smiler?'

'By the sea. I can see the sea…he, he's in his car…by the sea. They're coming.'

'Who's coming?'

'Help him!' Smiler yelled, his eyes wide and staring, his heels still beating against the floor. 'The noise.' He clapped his hands over his ears. 'The noise, please, please stop the noise, I can't stand it, please.'

Brother David reached out to try and calm him, but the next moment Smiler collapsed into a crumpled heap on the floor.

Deeply concerned for this boy he hardly knew, Brother David very carefully placed Smiler in the recovery position. He was just about to press the bell for a nurse when Detective Cox and Sergeant Rafferty entered the room.

'What's up?' Cox asked, hurrying to Smiler's side.

'Hello, Jason.' Brother David pointed at Smiler and sighed. 'He just suddenly started babbling. I couldn't understand half of what he was saying… Something about Mike being in danger?' He shook his head. 'Something about the sea. Whatever it is, he's really agitated. His whole body was shaking, like he was having a fit. Then he just sort of passed out.'

A moment later, Smiler moaned as he opened his eyes. Seeing Cox leaning over him, he grabbed the lapels on Cox's jacket and hauled himself up from the floor. 'It's Mike, they're gonna get him. Kill him. They'll kill him. Please, you have to help, they might already have done it. I can't see him… The pain, the pain… Help him. You have to help him.'

'OK, calm down.' Cox held up his hand. 'How do you know this? Who told you?'

Smiler was quiet for a moment, his body finally still. Then he looked Cox in the eye and said hesitantly, 'I…I see things, OK, believe me or not, it happens, I really can… It's frightening… And sometimes I hear things… I don't always know where it comes from, others do but I can't tell. Rita's the best at it.'

'It's OK, just calm down.' Cox lowered him onto the chair.

Sergeant Rafferty burst out laughing. 'Right nutter this one, all right.'

Sitting up straight in the chair as if he'd suddenly received an electric shock, Smiler then dropped his head, as Brother David said. 'There are more things in heaven----'

That was as far as he got. Cox, glaring at Rafferty, said, 'Right, Smiler, tell me what you know. Or,' he shrugged, 'whatever you think you can see.'

'Don't say you believe him?' Rafferty stared at Cox, her eyes wide in staged amazement.

'Let's just say I'm with Brother David on this, OK?' Turning back to Smiler, he said, 'Right, lad. What have you got to say for yourself? Quickly, please.'

But Rafferty turned to Brother David before Smiler had a chance to say anything. 'How can you, a priest, monk, or whatever the hell you are, believe in this shit?'

Brother David smiled as he replied, 'A very wise man once said, "Faith is taking the first step, even when you don't see the whole of the staircase".'

'Martin Luther King,' Smiler muttered, giving Brother David a twitch of a smile.

Impressed, and starting to think there was more to Smiler than he'd first thought, Cox said, 'OK. If Mike's in some sort of danger, we need to know now, Smiler, quick as you can.'

'Oh, please. What a waste of time. Can't you see the kid's obviously drugged up to the eyeballs? Or in desperate need of a fresh fix. Look how he's shaking. And you're prepared to believe him?' Shaking her head, Rafferty headed for the door. With a sarcastic sneer, she turned and said, 'I'll be in the car. But this is your call, nothing to do with me.'

'I'm fine with that.'

'OK, then.' Rafferty shrugged, as she walked out the door.

As if she'd never spoken, Smiler said, 'He's heading north, on the coast road. I can see the sea. It…it's as if I'm looking down at it.' Smiler started to shake even more, and clutched at his chest.

'It's OK, son. Just take your time,' Cox said.

Smiler stared at him for a moment, his eyes full of misery but tinged with a deep-seated belief. 'I don't know if it's already happened yet, or if it's going to happen, 'cos, 'cos I've never been confused like this before. I've told you before, it's Rita she knows everything. It's the noise. So much noise. It hurts. I…I feel dizzy as if I'm spinning in the air… I'm gonna be sick.' He clapped his hand over his mouth as he retched, staring at Cox, imploring him to believe him.

'Right. You're not making all that much sense, but I guess that's enough for me. Time we found out one way or another.' As Brother David handed a box of tissues to Smiler, Cox pulled out his phone. Within a few minutes he had three patrol cars out on the coast road, one coming down the coast road from the north, and two heading out of Berwick.

With a sigh, he snapped his phone shut, looked at Smiler and said, 'I hope you're right. In this age of government cuts we've just mobilised three already overworked vehicles.'

'I hope I'm not.' Smiler looked so down that it actually strengthened Cox's resolve. Ahh well, he thought, stranger things have happened.

Torn between wanting to stay with Aunt May and go in search of Mike, Smiler looked at Brother David.

Understanding his silent request, Brother David said, 'Go, go and find Mike. Don’t worry, I'll be here for her.' He patted Smiler's shoulder, and felt him flinch under the touch. The boy stepped to one side, and looked at Cox.

'Can I come?'

Cox hesitated for a moment, then thought, what the hell. Looking at smiler he said 'Don't see why not.'

CHAPTER SIX

Hands shaking, Mike struggled with the car, his heart was pounding enough to burst as he skidded ever closer to the edge of the cliff. Though he knew enough not to stamp on the brakes, he was still tempted. But the roads were wet from the earlier rain and slick with mud- a huge uncontrollable spin was highly possible. Everything was happening so fast, he barely had time to think. Between each breath it seemed the car skidded a different way.

He knew now that, unless a miracle happened in the next few minutes, he was going over the edge- and there was nothing he could do to save himself. His mind racing, he came up with a couple of ideas and just as quickly rejected them. Opening the car door and jumping out was not an option, he was on the wrong side of the car for that. Also, that was the side the bullet had entered and landing on it would probably kill him anyhow if the bullet was lodged somewhere internally. He could feel blood running down his side and pooling in the waistband of his jeans. The whole of his left side felt as if it was burning in hell.

Sweat broke out on his brow, and his heart flipped when the

nearside back wheel started to spin in mid air. He felt the car start to topple, then in a moment both front wheels were over the edge. Before he even had time to draw another breath, the whole car lifted and went over the cliff. He was airborne.

Mike clung on to the wheel as hard as he could, expecting at any moment to start spinning in the air. The miracle he'd asked for happened when the car did not turn over. All four wheels hit the ground, but the car started to waltz like some drunken learner at his first dance class. It lurched from side to side, until at last it righted itself. Mike took a deep breath, wondering if he dared hope...

It could straighten out.

Miracles do happen.

But a moment later, carried by momentum, the car started to slide. Slowly at first, then gathering speed. He could see the sea below him. The beautiful calmness he'd delighted in only minutes ago had turned into a monster ready to devour him.

'Shit, shit, shit,' he yelled. He was helpless, and guessed this was it. The end of the road for Mike Yorke.

Too soon.

Way too soon.

He had things to do, those murdering bastards deserved to die long before he did. And now they would get away with it.

Nothing would change, the world and everyone in it would go on getting screwed as it always had done.

Nothing I can do.

This is it!

Sharp, cold fear wrapped around his heart. A moment later, he bit into his tongue as what felt like a giant hand took hold of his head and slammed it into the side of the car. He was spinning now, spinning deeper and deeper into unconsciousness.

CHAPTER SEVEN

Detective Kristina Clancy was in the first car out of Berwick. She chewed on her lip as she and a young blonde woman police driver sped up the road.

Irritated, Kristina pulled at the lapel of her navy blue suit. As usual, she was impeccably dressed, matching her suit with a crisp white blouse. She could never get the right hand lapel of this suit to lie properly. It really annoyed the hell out of her. Then she fussed with her brown hair. Finally she gave up, tapping her long red fingernails on her knee, and admitted to herself the real reason she was so stressed out was Mike Yorke. She would love a cigarette, but she knew this driver would probably have a heart attack if she even hinted at it.

She and Mike went back a long way - once, when life was less complicated, they'd been an item. Working with him these last few weeks had brought it all back. She was starting to realise she was perhaps still in love with him, probably always had been, even through the short time of her marriage. Her husband, a good man, had died over a year ago. She'd asked for a transfer back to the north east to get away from his overbearing family who, though very kind and decent folk, thought she had to mourn forever. The problem was, she'd known within a week of being married that she didn't love him, that she'd probably married him on the rebound from Mike - although that hadn't stopped her from being absolutely gutted when he died.

The very last person she'd expected to be working with, when her transfer had finally come through, had been Mike, who usually worked out of Newcastle. She'd been quite shocked when she had seen his name on the rota on her first day.

Now, as her heart beat ever faster, she realised that yes, she did still love him, and this was probably the main reason why her marriage had failed.

What to do about it, though?

Or rather, what the hell can I do? As far as Mike's concerned, it was all over more than two years ago.

Sighing, she watched the green hills flashing by. Could there be another chance- or was she just chasing a dream?

'Where the hell can he be?' she muttered. Turning to the driver, she said, 'Slow down, we might be missing something. When we get to the top of this hill, stop, and we'll have a look around. He's got to be on this stretch of road.'

The driver nodded as she slowed the car down. 'So how do we know he's actually gone over? Surely if someone reported it, they would have stayed at the scene. I mean, come on, it's common sense, isn't it?'

Kristina sighed. 'Shame not everyone possesses it.'

'It's still a strange call, though, don't you think?'

'Yep, strange it is, and I'm beginning to suspect where it came from. Cox didn't give the whole story, just yelled over the phones that Mike Yorke was involved in an accident, and where he suspected that accident was.'

The driver frowned in puzzlement. She was about to ask more when Kristina hit the dashboard and yelled, 'Stop!'

'What?' She brought the car to a halt, noticing the mud on the road. There were tyre tracks in the mud at an impossible angle which led towards the edge of the road.

'That's gotta be him,' Kristina gasped.

“I sincerely hope not,' the driver said, opening her car door.

Oh God, Kristina thought as she jumped out of the car, please, please let him be all right.

Followed by the driver, she ran to the edge, every second fearing what she might find - if it was indeed even Mike.

CHAPTER EIGHT

Sergeant Angela Rafferty scowled as she started the car. 'What on earth are you thinking of, taking us on a wild goose chase because that little toe rag insists he's a psychic? You'll be asking him for the lottery numbers next.'

'He is with us, you know.'

Rafferty looked in the rear view mirror at Smiler. 'You sure about that?'

Cox turned in his seat. Smiler was sitting perfectly still with his eyes closed. Turning back, Cox said, 'Just get a move on.'

'What the----?' she demanded a moment later. She kept throwing quick looks in the rear view mirror and frowning even more at Smiler, who now looked as if every single muscle in his body was dancing.

Glancing at her and seeing where her attention was, Cox spun round, looked at Smiler, and shook his head. Turning back, he went on, 'When you've been in this game as long as I have, you'll learn not to judge until you have all the facts. Brother David was right to quote Martin Luther King.'

'Whatever.'

Again, Cox wondered why she had such an attitude, and how she'd even managed to make it to detective. She's only been with us a couple of weeks, and already she struts around behaving as if she despises everyone she comes into contact with, as well as owning the flaming place. He had actually tried to check her out on the internet, but, strangely, he'd thought at the time, he could find no trace at all of her having been in any other police force.

Hearing Smiler start muttering, he looked round at him. 'Smiler…Smiler, you all right, son?' His voice rose as Smiler started to thrash around.

'For God's sake, what's wrong with him?' Rafferty asked.

'How the hell should I know?' Cox snapped.

They came over the hill, and fifty yards down Rafferty saw a police car pulled over on the opposite side of the road. 'Looks like they've found something.' She flicked her siren on. As she did so, a woman's head popped over the edge.

'It's Kristina,' Cox said. 'Looks like she's standing on a ledge or something.'

'He's gonna fall,' Smiler said, in a matter of fact voice. 'He is…He's gonna fall right into the sea.' He started nodding his head, then counting on his fingers.

Another glance over his shoulder, and Cox could see that Smiler was staring out of the window. Apart from the constant muttering and quick-time counting on his fingers, he seemed calmer than a few minutes ago.

Cox had acted on a hunch, having truly seen some things that had no explanation at all in his time in the police force. He had only hoped that his hunch to trust Smiler would prove correct - and it certainly looked like it had.

Cox opened the car door as they came to a halt, practically bumper to bumper with the other police car.

'Jason,' Kristina yelled, as Cox came into view around the car. 'He's here.'

Smiler quickly got out of the car, tripped a few times in his hurry, but reached the edge at the same time as Cox.

'Hi, Smiler. I'm guessing from what I've been told that you're responsible for getting us here.'

Smiler nodded. 'Is he…is he all right?'

Kristina sighed, and shook her head. 'It's impossible to tell. Take a look. No one can get down there without the proper equipment. I've phoned for fire engines and an ambulance, they should be here any minute.'

Heart pounding, Smiler looked over the edge, dreading what he would find. Kristina and the blonde policewoman were standing on a wide ledge about five feet down. From there, it was a steep slope for about forty feet - although quite dangerous for anyone, it was certainly passable for people trained for this kind of rescue. Then it was a sheer drop to the beach. Halfway down the slope, Mike's car was wedged between two young trees that were swaying and bending dangerously.

'You have to get him out of there, he's not dead, you have to get him out!' Smiler's voice rose with each word until he was shouting. 'He's hurt, but he's alive, I, I can feel him.' He started laughing hysterically. 'I can feel him!'

'It's OK, lad,' Cox said soothingly, but he was thinking, no way could anyone live through that. The car was squashed on both sides and the roof rose up and down like waves on a high sea.

Kristina held up her hand, interrupting Cox. 'Here's the fire engines, thank God.'

Then they all heard them. She's got damn good ears, Cox was thinking, as two fire engines appeared over the brow of the hill.

CHAPTER NINE

Brother David rested his forehead on the side of the bed beside Aunt May's arm. Opening one eye, he watched the life-giving liquid drip into her veins. He was all out of prayers. He didn't know what hurt the most, his heart or his soul. Within twenty-four hours, the three people he loved had all been placed in deadly danger. He didn't know what game Tony was playing, but in his heart he knew he couldn't be a part of what was going on. He knew him too well. And he guessed Mike didn't really believe it either, no matter what the evidence.

He stood up, stretching his neck and shoulders to ease the stiffness as he slowly walked to the window. A noise behind him caused him to spin round. 'Oh, my dear God… She's woken up! Thank you. Thank you.'

His heart, which had soared, plummeted once more into the depths. It was just a nurse, one he'd never seen before. She said, 'Why don't you go and get something to eat?'

Brother David shook his head. 'No thank you. I really don't want to leave her alone.'

'I promise I'll stay till you get back. You must be starving. She'll need you to keep your strength up.'

Brother David sighed. He could go without food, but he needed to drink. He'd seen first-hand the effects of dehydration.

'OK. I'll have something quick. Promise you won't leave her? I don't want her to wake up and think she's all alone.'

'Honestly, there's no hurry.' She smiled at him. 'The café is on the bottom floor, near the entrance. Just take the lift and turn right, you can't miss it.'

'Thank you.' Brother David nodded.

He was just about to go through the door when the doctor came in. Seeing Brother David's eyes light up, he said, 'Sorry, it's just a routine check.'

'OK, Doctor. Just going for a cuppa, then.' He hurried out, planning to be back in less than ten minutes, just enough time to grab a drink and a sandwich or two, and bring them back up to the room with him.

The doctor entered the room, nodding at the nurse, wondering who this one was. He'd certainly never seen her before. Quite a looker, he thought, smiling at her as he reached the bed.

CHAPTER TEN

The fire chief carefully tied the rope around the officer's waist, and gave it one more hefty tug before slapping him on the back and saying, 'Go get him, Jack.'

Jack nodded with a smile and, watched anxiously by the chief and everyone there, he was slowly, step by tortured step, lowered down the muddy bank.

Kristina dug her nails into the palms of her hands, then pushed her knuckles into her mouth as Jack finally, after what seemed a very long time, reached the car. Easing round crabwise, he went to the front of the car first.

It was obvious to those watching that he could see nothing inside. Most of the bonnet had replaced the windshield. Being careful not to touch anything - any sudden movement could send the car and Mike down to the beach below, and probably him with it - Jack moved slowly round to the driver's side, where he disappeared for what seemed forever. Kristina's heart nearly froze as she silently begged him to hurry up. Then just as she was about to lose all hope Jack's head popped up.

'Yes!' she yelled, punching the sky as he gave a thumbs-up sign. It was smiles all round as everyone started to clap. The fire-man was winched back up to them, where he was given a final pull over the edge by Cox on one hand, and the fire chief on the other.

Smiler swallowed hard as he stared down at the car. Hang on Mike, hang on, he was thinking, as hard as he could, trying in his own way to reach him and let him know that they were there. But he could sense nothing. Where Mike usually rested in his head, there was nothing but an empty space.

'OK, Jack, you've assessed the damage - any ideas on how we can fix it?' the fire chief asked.

'Well.' Jack looked from his chief to Kristina, who noticed a slight tic at the side of his mouth. Then he went on. 'I really can't tell a hundred percent if he's dead or unconscious. There's blood, but I can't see where it's coming from, or if it's a serious wound or not. It's still trickling out from somewhere, though, which I think is a good sign. I honestly think the only way we can get him to safety, is by winching the car up using both fire engines. And it'll be tricky, 'cause the soil is unstable. Any harsh movement could easily set off a landslide. But it would be practically impossible to get in and get him out, where he is now. It's just not safe, we have to get him up here inside the car.'

Kristina, watched intently by Smiler, clutched at the fire chief's jacket. 'Is…will he be all right?'

Waiting for his reply, Kristina chewed on her thumbnail.

Before she could say anything else, the fire chief patted her back. 'Don't worry, we'll get him up. Trust me - we've done trickier jobs than this.'

She nodded, as she thought, Yes, but will he be alive?

Is he dying this minute?

Smiler looked from the fire chief, to Kristina, then down at the car. He was thinking exactly the same thing.

CHAPTER ELEVEN

Prince Carl, tall, slim, and with a fine shock of dark hair was, although reasonably good looking, not quite as handsome as he liked to believe. His very large nose made sure of that. He was descended not from the Russian Romanov royal family, but from the 12th century Golitsyn royal house, on his mother's side.

On his way to meet Count Rene Farqahar, he paused for a moment and stared up at the magnificent Chartres Cathedral. Count Rene had a house in town, and was practically the only member of the Families that he called friend, although he was on speaking terms with most of them. They gossiped frequently about the others, even though it was not supposed to be allowed. They both guessed, rightly, that they were not, nor ever had been, the only ones to do so.

He loved Chartres, especially the cathedral, and never missed a chance to stare at the famous blue stained glass windows. His castle was five miles away, hidden from view by the countless trees that surrounded it. He shared his time between France and the homeland he shared with Kirill Tarasov, Russia.

It was such a lovely day that Prince Carl decided not to take another taxi, but to walk the mile or so to Count Rene's house. He gloried in nodding at people he knew, amused that they did not have a clue as to what the world was really about, and the fact that he was one of their masters. When on walkabout he loved to dress casually in jeans and open neck shirts, mostly white. It increased his feeling of power. This was one of the reasons he liked to leave the car at home and take a taxi into town, so he could indulge.

Twenty minutes later, he rang the bell on the door of Count Rene's town house. In a matter of moments, the door was opened by Count Rene himself.

Prince Carl frowned in surprise. This was very unusual. Rene did nothing at all for himself, he had a servant for everything. Prince Carl had once, as they were sharing a few drinks together, accused him of even having a servant to wipe his arse. Rene had merely laughed, and hadn't denied it.

'Come in, come in,' Count Rene said, stepping back and ushering Prince Carl into the splendid hallway.

A manservant came from the far end, obviously to open the door, and was as surprised as Prince Carl had been. When Count Rene snarled at him, he swiftly turned and disappeared back through a door at the far end of the hallway,

Prince Carl followed him into the large, lavishly furnished drawing room. Count Rene pointed to a seat, by the fireplace, which was still heaped with logs though, in this heat, unlit. A huge mirror dominated the chimneybreast, and dotted around the room were life-sized white marble statues of angels, some with their wings spread as if ready to take flight, and others with their wings closed and their heads bowed in a praying posture. Prince Carl looked at the room through the mirror. He smiled at the ceiling rose, solid gold back-to-back unicorns. It was the trademark of the Families.

'The usual, Carl?' Count Rene asked, from the well stocked bar that ran the length of the west wall.

'Why not. So, I see you're growing a beard again. What have you been doing in public this ti---- Ah, that's why you're here in midsummer, and not at your mansion in the south.' Prince Carl laughed. 'You've been up to your old tricks again.'

Count Rene handed him a tumbler of whiskey and, sitting in a chair by the fireplace, crossed his legs and said, 'Nothing special. The police chief suggested it would be best to lie low for a few months until he manages to make certain that one or two trivial items disappear off the radar.'

Prince Carl shook his head. 'You know, Rene, there are some things we just shouldn't do. It's nowhere near as easy to control information now, not with this fucking Facebook, and all the other internet sites. Word can get around the planet in minutes.'

'What can they say, for God's sake? One or two have come close, but it's easily been laughed off as a conspiracy theory, you know that. And that's why what is planned for the big twelve next year has to happen. You're right - we can get away with murder, and just about everything else, but we never had to go into hiding, and it will get worse. It was, if you remember, foreseen.' He scowled, before going on, 'You and others of your thinking are going to rob us of our birthright.'

Prince Carl stubbornly shook his head. 'It can't happen.' He took the glass of whiskey from Count Rene's hand and took a long swallow. After putting the glass on a side table, he went on, 'Times have changed, Rene.'

'Only because you, that idiot Tarasov and a few others are willing to let them. It's all right for him, stuck in fucking Siberia, where he lives the life our ancestors lived. Getting his kicks by shoving people out naked into below 50 degree temperatures, watching them freeze to death, delighting in the death crystals they produce with their last breath, before having them hauled into his huge larder.'

'Beats going to Iceland,' Prince Carl sniggered.

Count Rene snorted. 'That's got to be the first time I've ever heard you make even an attempt at a joke! Please don't ever attempt another one. But that aside, I've got to know you will back us for the Glorious Twelfth.'

'No. We have got to learn to adapt. Time to leave the peasant Neanderthals alone.'

'It's called progress.'

Prince Carl snorted. 'It's called unnecessary suffering. And I for one can't see the need.'

'So, who cares. They've mostly fulfilled their function - now we need time to let the planet breathe.'

Prince Carl sighed. 'We can still mostly do whatever we want. I really don't see the need for it. We've already thinned them out with two world wars and various plagues. Plus, think about it. the fewer there are of them, the fewer consumers we'll have. Can't you damn well see that?'

Count Rene shook his head. 'You know, they are breeding far quicker than was predicted. Already they're eating their way around the planet like a herd of fucking locusts. If this goes on, soon there will be no resources left.'

'Nonsense. You know fine well that global warming was set up as a conspiracy theory. It worked, as well.'

'So you won't back me?'

'No.'

There was silence between them for a while, both of them realising that their friendship had run its course. Prince Carl rose from his chair. He nodded at Count Rene, who dropped his head and gave one nod. Prince Carl made for the door and let himself out.

CHAPTER TWELVE

Listening to the fire chief giving his order, Cox suddenly said, 'Bloody hell, where's Smiler?' Standing next to him Rafferty, wearing a frown that said, Who cares? shrugged.

Cox hurried back to the car. At first glance it looked like no one was inside. Opening the back door, he saw Smiler crouched in a ball on the floor, crying his eyes out.

'What's up, kid?' Cox asked.

Smiler looked up, tears running down his face, trapped in the deep smile lines carved at each side of his mouth.

'Rita says he's all right.' He heaved a sigh of relief, as he tried to wipe the tears away. 'He is. If Rita says he's all right, he really, really is. She knows.'

'Who's Rita?'

'She...she's a friend. She can see loads better than me, she knows when things are happening. I'm never sure if they're happening now, gonna happen or already have. She says his spark is burning bright.'

Cox puffed out his cheeks, shrugged, and said, 'OK, if Rita

says he's all right, who am I to argue with her?'

'Technically Rita's a him. She's a transvestite, she likes dressing in women's clothes----'

Cox held his hand up. 'I know what a transvestite is, thanks. Met more than one. And I know the difference between a transvestite and a drag queen. My opinion? It's up to them. So let's get you out of here, lad.' As he moved his hand down to help Smiler, he was thinking, this whole bloody thing just gets weirder and weirder. He said, 'Come on then, sunshine, move it.'

Hesitatingly, Smiler held out his hand for Cox to help him up thinking, Get a grip, get a grip, behaving like a fucking girl! He ground his teeth together.

Seven years old was the last time Smiler had cried. He'd vowed then, when the man had wiped his tears with a grin on his face, and walked away without looking back, never to cry again. He'd managed just fine up till now. It was good not to feel, easier to survive. And then he'd met Mike, and everything changed. Now he could feel, but now he could also hurt…again.

Once out of the car, Smiler started rambling, 'I can't see him, but Rita can. Rita says he's fine.'

Having seen the state of the car and heard what the fireman had to say, Cox doubted this very much. But he said, 'So, er - tell me more about this Rita.'

Smiler sighed, but it was an impatient sigh, dredged up by the memories he'd just had. He snapped, ' Friggin' hell… Rita lives in

London, she knows a lot of things, if she says she can see Mike, then she can. OK?'

'See him how?'

'In her mind, of course, where else?' Smiler looked at Cox as if he was an idiot. 'I can't tell the difference if they are in a coma or unconscious or dead… They sort of just go away.' He clenched his fists to stop them from trembling, clinging faithfully to what Rita had told him, starting to get slightly edgy from the fact that this copper who he hardly knew seemed to doubt him.

'So where's Rita now?' Cox asked.

'In London.'

'Phone you, did she?'

'No.'

'Am I missing something?'

Smiler glared at him from under his eyelids, and stubbornly refused to be drawn into any more question and answer sessions.

Too nosy, this one. He might be one of Mike's friends, but he also might be after something else.

By this time they had reached the edge. They looked over and watched as two firemen, both tied to an engine, and each of them carrying a winching cable, very carefully, inch by inch, made their way down the rocky slope.

The fireman on the left reached the car a couple of seconds before the other one. Deftly he slipped the cable under the front axle, looped it over and clipped it together. Giving the thumbs up to the other fireman, he tugged on his rope and slowly, with help from above, began to make his way back up. Once he was out of the way, the second fireman moved in.

Glancing at Smiler, and noticing his grim, set face, Cox said, 'Stop worrying, kid, the worst's over. Ten minutes, tops.'

Smiler turned to look at him. His expression sent shivers down Cox's spine, and what he said next did not help.

Shaking his head, Smiler said slowly, 'No… It's just begun.'

CHAPTER THIRTEEN

There was one nerve-wracking moment, when they all held their breath as the car got stuck in a small avalanche of soil. The firemen, jumping back down as if they were abseiling down the side of a building, managed to move it carefully away with their bare hands. Everyone was desperately praying that their actions would not start a bigger avalanche. The firemen were again hauled up to the road, then the final operation to get the car up, and Mike free, began.

At first it was inch by slow inch while everyone watched in fear, holding hands. The ten minutes that it took seemed to drag on and on. Then, amidst cheers, the car was finally pulled onto the road.

Smiler was the first one to the door. With a struggle, and a whole lot of determination, he managed to pull it open.

'Mike.'

Kristina, standing right behind Smiler, echoed Mike's name. Neither of them received an answer. Kristina's hand went to her mouth, her eyes welling up with tears. Mike wasn't moving. Please

God, please, she prayed, let him be alive.

Smiler was frozen to the spot, his eyes wide in horror, convinced now that Rita had made a mistake. Stepping between them, Cox placed his fingers on Mike's pulse. After a moment, his smile slowly spread. 'He's alive, thank God.'

'What?' Smiler gulped before echoing Cox. 'He's alive?'

Still smiling, Cox nodded.

Katrina wanted to jump in the air. Her heart racing, she said, 'You're sure?'

Smiler swung his gaze back to Cox, waiting for more confirmation.

Cox nodded. 'Yep, he'll be around to torment us for a long time yet.' He lifted his hand to pat Smiler's shoulder, thought better of it and said, 'Looks like your friend Rita was right after all.'

Smiler gave him a slow, satisfied nod.

Cox moved over for the paramedic, a young man with a blond beard and moustache and the most startling green eyes, who placed his fingers on the same pulse as Cox. After a moment, he nodded, then started checking Mike out, while his partner - a middle aged woman with a friendly smile- and another fireman brought a stretcher over. By this time, two of the other firemen had taken the door off the car, making plenty of room for people to reach Mike safely.

'We'll have to move him to find out where the blood's coming from,' said the young paramedic. 'I'm pretty sure he's knocked himself out by hitting his head on the door. But it's the blood I'm worried about. His vital signs are strong, though.'

Everyone hastily moved away to give the paramedics a chance to do their job. As they put him on the stretcher, Mike groaned. He opened his eyes, looked right at Smiler and, after a moment, winked. Smiler's heart skipped a beat. Rita was right!

Wishing the wink had been for her, Kristina climbed in to the ambulance behind Mike, telling the paramedics that she was Mike's partner, which was true - only, not in the way that they believed. Smiler put his foot on the first step of the ambulance, only to be held back by a restraining hand from the first paramedic, who had taken Mike's pulse and declared him alive. Smiler refused to move.

'Sorry, but family only,' the paramedic said.

'I am family,' Smiler replied determinedly.

Seeing the stubborn look on Smiler's face, he relented and, shaking his head, turned back to Mike. 'OK, let's see what we've got here. Can you turn over onto your right side, please, and we'll see where the blood's coming from.'

Smiler, who had no love for the sight of blood, hastily looked away as the man helped Mike to roll over.

When he lifted Mike's t-shirt, the paramedic said, 'Oh. Nasty.'

'What?' Mike asked, trying to wriggle around to see, but Kristina grabbed his hand and, touching his face, said, 'No, Mike, please- leave it to them.'

Frowning, he asked, 'How bad is it?'

Smiler held his breath, waiting for the paramedic's answer, begging any God up there who would listen for Mike to be all right.

'Actually,' the young man said, with a smile, 'it's nowhere near as bad as it looks. The bullet's grazed along the side, and made a groove about seven inches long, but it's all surface. It's the length of it that's caused so much blood. You're gonna be fine, mate, once we get you out of here and into the hospital.'

'You always were a lucky bugger,' Kristina grinned. 'Did you see who did it, recognise anyone?'

Gently looking into her eyes, Mike removed Kristina's hand from his face. Registering the slight momentary hurt in her eyes, he looked quickly away. Kristina was a complication he certainly didn't need at this time. To be close to him meant danger for everyone concerned.

'No.'

His tone had been deliberately harsh. He went on in the same manner, while Smiler frowned at him, 'Neither did I recognise the car, or even see the friggin' colour, before you ask. It all happened too damn fast, OK?'

Turning to the paramedic, he said, 'Lousy headache. Have you got anything for it?'

'We'll be at the hospital in three minutes, mate. They'll sort you.'

'I'm not going in.'

The paramedic swung round to face Kristina and raised his eyebrows in an expression that said, Help me out here.

Kristina stared at Mike for a moment before saying, 'You have to go in to the hospital, Mike, you've had a nasty bang on your head. It needs looking at. Plus, that wound is still bleeding-you could end up with all sorts of infections if you leave it.'

'I'll live.'

'You're just being pig-headed now.'

'She's right,' the paramedic nodded.

'Yes, she is,' Smiler added.

Mike swung his head to Smiler and glowered at him. 'Did I ask for your input? Go on get yourself back to London where you belong. You're nothing but a friggin' nuisance, anyhow.'

Smiler gasped, as Mike turned away from him.

As the ambulance came to a stop, Mike jumped up and was at the door before any of them.

Stepping in front of him, the paramedic said, as the doors were opening, 'I really do think you need to get that wound looked at, and you need your head seeing to.'

Katrina couldn't help but smile. The paramedic, noticing this, realised what he'd said. 'Oh… I didn't mean it that way. Sorry.' Looking away, he grinned to himself.

'Just get me the forms to sign, will you? I'm outta here.' Ignoring Kristina and Smiler, who both kept insisting that he stayed, he stepped down from the ambulance.

Having arrived a couple of minutes earlier, Cox was standing at the bottom of the steps and had heard everything.

'You will stay, Mike, and that's an order!' Immediately Cox regretted what he'd said. Orders were the wrong way to go with Mike. But he had to follow through. 'It's in the rule book, Mike- if anything should happen when you're on duty... Anyhow, you know all this, don't you?'

Mike gritted his teeth. He knew that Cox was right, but he needed to get away now while the trail was still there. He looked down at his shoes, but he was seeing the car, the blue car with the number plate SHE 971.

'OK. But once the check's over, I'm off.'

Behind him, Smiler heaved a sigh of relief and Katrina put her hand on Mike's arm. Shaking her hand off, with an impatient gesture, he strode into the hospital.

CHAPTER FOURTEEN

Watching Mike go, Smiler seized the opportunity to quickly visit Aunt May. As he rushed past the cafeteria, he remembered that he'd had nothing at all to eat since breakfast time. His stomach rumbled as he smelt food.

Should I grab something now? he thought. Mike's gonna be ages yet, 'cause he'll probably have to have x-rays and stuff. His stomach rumbled again.

Ham sandwich it is, I guess. Hope they don't have them all smothered with mayonnaise. Why do they do that?

He checked his pockets and came up with seven pounds in change. Might be enough for two, 'cause Brother David hasn't had anything either. Shit - neither has Mike.

'Guess it's crisps all round, then,' he muttered.

Turning in mid stride, he was passing through the doors when a black shadow seemed to float in front of him, making his vision blurred, and thickening quickly whichever way he looked. He stepped closer, and it grew even thicker. The hairs on the back of his neck stood up. Seriously freaked out, Smiler backed away and the vision faded, moved forward again and it grew back.

'OK, so it's obvious, whatever it is, it doesn't want me going in there. So where does it want me to go, and why?' he mumbled at the slowly swirling blackness, receiving a strange look from a nurse who quickly squeezed past him.

'Oh, friggin' hell,' he said a moment later, all hunger forgotten. 'Aunt May!'

He ran for the stairs, bypassing the lift as there were at least ten people waiting. Taking the stairs two at a time, he reached Aunt May's floor in a few minutes. He raced along the corridor, slowing as he came to her room. Stopping before anyone inside could see him, he cautiously peeped around the door.

Where's Brother David? he thought with a frown, as he saw a nurse he hadn't seen before. She had dark curly hair and a stocky but shapely figure, and it looked like she was filling a syringe up from a small bottle she had taken out of her pocket.

What's that for? Smiler wondered.

Reaching for one of the tubes, the nurse was about to inject the contents of the bottle when Smiler walked through the door and said, 'What are you doing?'

She turned quickly and frowned at him. 'What's it got to do with you? Go away.'

'I've never seen you before. Who are you, and where's her regular nurse?'

Staring at her, Smiler felt his heart beat begin to quicken.

There was something quite wrong here, he sensed it - his skin felt as if it was crawling over his body. Frightened, but determined to protect Aunt May whatever the cost, he moved forward until he was standing at the end of the bed. In his typically blunt way, he repeated, 'So who are you? You're definitely not the regular nurse, 'cause I've never seen you before.'

Still standing with the syringe in her hand, she replied, 'Obviously I am a nurse, and who are you?'

'She's my Aunt May, OK, and I'm gonna get the doc.'

'I wouldn't if I were you.'

'Why, what you gonna do to stop me?' As he asked the question Smiler was shaking inside, even though he was putting on quite a swagger as he moved closer. Her dark eyes were piercing right through him. He'd seen eyes like that before, on the streets, when all hope had gone, eyes with no soul. The bearer of those eyes was capable of anything.

Praying he could keep it together, and without thinking it through, he quickly moved around the side of the bed. At the same moment, she leapt over the bed, a knife held high in her hand. Smiler grabbed a vase of yellow roses from the bedside cabinet and threw them at her. Ducking, she dropped the syringe but held onto the knife. Dripping wet, her arms covered in thorns from the roses, she screamed, and was about to lunge again when a deep voice stopped her in her tracks.

'What the----?' said Brother David from the doorway. As

Smiler stood in front of the tubes that were attached to Aunt May, he was prepared to defend her as best he could, but breathed a sigh of relief when Brother David appeared, so much bigger than he- and so much bigger than the nurse.

Taking the opportunity of Brother David's surprise entry, she swung quickly around Smiler, and before he could react she was gone.

CHAPTER FIFTEEN

'Can you tell me what she looked like?' Cox asked Smiler. 'Think hard.' They were sitting in one of the offices on the top floor of the hospital, each of them nursing a cup of coffee, while Aunt May -- still unaware of anything that was going on around her - was being transferred, with two guards, to a more secure room on the other side of the building.

Tearing the wrapper off a cheese and pickle sandwich that Brother David had brought back for him, Smiler described the woman in as much detail as he could. Brother David agreed, adding a three inch tattoo on her calf that Smiler had missed.

'So, what sort of tattoo?' Cox asked, as Brother David swivelled round in his chair- the setting sun was glaring into his eyes. He moved the chair closer to Cox.

'It was just a glance. I thought it was blood at first. I think it was an animal, some sort of horse, only a lot of red in it, black writing inside of the horse and on the outside. That's about it, really, except... I'm not sure, mind, but I think there might have been two horses, both of them standing on their back legs, sort of back to back. She was very quick, too. Never seen anyone scramble so quickly before, she's obviously very athletic.'

'Either of you seen her around the hospital before?'

Smiler looked at Brother David and shrugged. Brother David shook his head. Smiler, having devoured one of the sandwiches that Brother David had brought back for him, the other still in his hand, stood up and started edging towards the door. 'Can I go now? I really want to see Aunt May and Mike.'

Cox rubbed his chin. 'Hmm. Yeah, sure. Just one thing, and I know this is a stupid question, but can anyone think of a reason why someone should want to hurt Aunt May? There have now been two attempts on her life in the past twenty-four hours. Rather strange, don't you think?'

'No one she knows, that's definite. Not a better person alive in the whole world, anyone will tell you that. But you already know this, Jason, you've met her a few times… Perhaps it's something that she knows,' Brother David said.

Smiler hung his head. Looking at him, Cox frowned before asking, 'What else do you know, Smiler? After all, you were right about Mike being in danger.'

'Nothing… I don't know any more than what I said.' But Smiler had spoken far too quickly for Cox's liking. Not for nothing did Mike call him the Ferret.

'So explain how you knew Mike was, for all intents and purposes, hanging off the edge of a cliff. I mean, it's not something a lot of us can do, is it?'

'What, hang off the edge of a cliff? Easy,' Smiler snapped.

'You know what I mean, Smiler.'

Smiler sighed. 'Rita. It was Rita, most times it's…Rita. She's been at it for a long time. Much longer than me. She knows a lot. Me, I'm just a learner.'

'Most times? Does this happen often?'

Smiler shrugged. 'You don't need to know. Mike's right, he says the less anyone knows the safer you'll be.' Smiler was becoming very uncomfortable with all the questions and, anxious to see both Aunt May and Mike, he moved to the doorway.

'Smiler?' Brother David said. 'Where are you going?'

'Mind your own business,' he suddenly snapped. 'It's got nothing to do with you.' He spun round to Cox. 'And you neither, so fuck off, both of you.' Quickly he left them and headed downstairs.

'What the----?' Cox frowned.

Brother David shrugged, and held out his hands, palm up. 'Mike said he gets like that sometimes.'

Cox sighed. 'No one in the hospital fits the description you gave me earlier. Well, actually a couple come close, but they all have concrete alibis for the time. One was in the operating theatre, and the other was on the kids' ward, entertaining half a dozen of them. We can only assume it's something to do with this business that Mike wants to keep to himself.'

'And we all know how stubborn he can be when he wants to.'

Cox smiled. 'Too right.'

'OK, if you're finished with me?'

'Certainly. I'll pop along later, see how she's getting on.'

'Right then. I'll be off.'

CHAPTER SIXTEEN

'Look, I know you want to get out of here,' the doctor said, 'but you have had a severe knock to your head. My advice is to stay in overnight at least, so that we can keep an eye on you. A blow to the head can be very dangerous, and sometimes even hours later the consequences can be devastating.'

'Thanks, Doc,' Mike muttered.

The doctor held up his hand and quickly said, 'Not that I'm saying anything is going to happen, mind you, just that it's always best to be on the safe side.'

Mike chewed it over, knowing that the doctor was right, and that he personally would call anyone a fool for ignoring the advice. 'OK, one night. First light, I'm outta here.'

The doctor smiled his relief. 'So, if you would just rest now… I can give you something to help you relax, if you need it.'

'No thank you!'

'OK.' The doctor was just about to leave the room when Smiler came in.

'Hi, Mike. You all right, then?'

'Yes.'

Feeling awkward and obviously unwelcome, Smiler sighed and stared at his feet. Why was Mike doing this?

The doctor could sense the tension in the room. His job here done, he decided to leave them alone. 'OK then, I'll be off. I'm glad you've seen sense and decided to stay, it's mostly a precaution. You should be perfectly fine after a good night's sleep.'

Staring at Smiler, Mike grunted an answer and, shrugging, the doctor left, muttering under his breath, 'Bloody patients, know it all, they think they do.'

Ignoring him, Mike said, 'Why are you still here?'

'Why are you being such a fucking pain in the arse?' Smiler retorted.

This brought a twitch of a smile to Mike's lips. He thought about it before saying, 'Right, Smiler, you know why, you're far from friggin' stupid. But I'll spell it out for you, yes? This is the first attempt on my life, and it won't be the last. You know this, and I don't need you or bloody Rita to tell me, OK?'

'You should listen, Mike. Rita knows what she's talking about,' Smiler muttered.

'To hell with Rita. It's a load of friggin' rubbish. How many times do I have to tell you, for God's sake? Get it through your thick head, it's all a coincidence.'

'It's not,' Smiler replied stubbornly. ' Your mind is too closed, Mike, you only ever see everyday things. And there is no such thing as coincidence.'

Mike shook his head in exasperation. 'Again, how many times do I have to say it? I don't believe in your mumbo jumbo. I've told you till I'm fucking sick of telling you... I do not want any of you hurt through being close to me. I am truly sorry if I've hurt your feelings, but it's the only way to get through to you. For your own good, I do not want you around me. Any of you,' he added, his eyes narrowing as Kristina and Cox walked in the door.

'I've ordered extra guards for you and your Aunt May, Mike. Should help you get a night's sleep, at least,' Cox said. 'Are you feeling any better?'

Mike nodded. 'Yes, and thanks.' Although sleep was the last thing on his mind, he knew that he needed it, would have to have it. He had to be fresh for what was coming.

'There's also guards on the entrance, plus a half dozen or so scattered around the hospital. Anyone behaving the least bit suspiciously will be stopped at once.'

'Just make sure she's all right, that's all I ask.'

Cox looked him in the eye. 'You know we'll do our best. But you, what do you plan on doing tomorrow?'

'Like he's gonna tell us,' Smiler butted in.

Gently putting her hand on Smiler's arm, Kristina shushed him.

As if Smiler had never spoken, Mike said to Cox, 'Can't say, but I'll keep in touch.' He swung his face towards Kristina, and felt a small stab in his heart. She had re-awoken feelings he thought he had lost forever.

Bad timing, kiddo. For the foreseeable future, my life's on hold.

'How can I help?' Kristina asked.

'You can't.'

'Please, Mike.' She moved to the side of his bed. 'Don't shut me out, not now.'

But Mike refused to look at her. Staring at the wall, he said, 'Can't you see? I have no choice. When I get to the bottom of this, if I think it's safe to involve you, I will. All of you.'

'But----'

Mike ignored her. As if she'd never spoken, he said. 'Go away…All of you.'

Cox heaved a loud sigh, and they all turned to him. 'It seems that I know the least. What I do know is that if you say it's dangerous for us all, then I believe you, and whatever you want me to do, you just have to say the word.'

'I know I can trust everyone in here. But believe me, none of you know who you can trust. So please believe me when I say, trust no one but each other. And that's it, you're getting no more from me.'

'But Mike…' Kristina said. 'We're your friends, we need to know what we're up against.'

Grim faced Smiler nodded.

'Are you all fucking thick or what?' Mike yelled. 'How many times do I have to tell you?'

'Could you please keep the noise down in here there are other patients to consider.' The nurse said as she came into the room.

Mike looked at the three of them in turn, before saying 'Go!'

Slowly Smiler backed out of the room, followed by a deflat- ed Kristina and a frowning Cox.

PART TWO

CHAPTER SEVENTEEN

Petrified, holding her breath, Shelly stood as still as she could. In each hand she held a wire coat hanger, her face an inch from the inside of the wardrobe door. She heard the door to her room open. A soft footfall, and she knew he was in the room. Silence for a moment, in which she pictured him looking around for her, then another soft footfall and he was outside the wardrobe door. She could hear him breathing, smell the cigarette he had just smoked.

What if he suddenly starts shooting?

He's gonna open this door sooner than later.

Oh God, please help me.

Shaking inside, fear mounting by the second, she squeezed her hands tightly around the hangers. Praying that he was facing the door, Shelly did the only thing she could think of.

Bursting out of the wardrobe, arms held high, she brought them both down together. The point of the left coat hanger lodged deeply into the bottom of the man's right eye, and the right coat hanger went into his mouth. Yanking downwards with all the strength she could muster, she ripped open his eye and tore off a piece of his gum.

Screaming, the man dropped his gun and clutched at his face, blood pouring through his fingers as he desperately tried to keep his eyeball in place while spitting out a chunk of bloody flesh with a tooth attached.

Shelly grabbed the gun with one hand, her bag with the other, hesitated for a split second while she glared at the man who had planned to murder her. Lifting her right foot, she booted him as hard as she could and sent him sprawling across the floor.

'Bastard!' she screamed, with a brief feeling of satisfaction, shoving the gun into her bag. Then, knowing that time was her enemy, she made it out of the hospital as fast as she could.

An hour later she was sitting in the cab of a lorry heading down the A1. The driver, a short, blond, middle aged man, seemed a decent sort and had talked about nothing but his family since she had sat down. Shelly was impatient to get as far away as she could, as quickly as she could, knowing that the hunt for her had probably started within minutes of her escape.

'So how long before we get to Manchester?' Shelly interrupted his monologue about his seven year old daughter Mia, who he obviously adored.

He glanced at the clock on the dashboard, and said, 'Just over an hour, love, very little traffic this early on a morning. In a hurry, like?'

'Sort of.'

'Well, don't worry. You'll have no problems at all hitching another lift from where I'll drop you, a good looking chick like you.' He winked at her.

Shelly sat upright in her seat, the alarm bells inside springing to action.

Keep calm, keep calm, could just be an innocent comment, she told herself, crossing her legs and staring out of the window. He surely can't be one of them?

'Smoke?' he asked. Keeping one hand on the wheel, he handed her a packet of cigarettes, gently brushing down the back of her hand with his finger.

CHAPTER EIGHTEEN

Mike woke up, surprised that he'd managed to sleep at all. He stretched, then jumped in shock as a voice said, 'All right now?'

Mike spun round. 'Smiler, for God's sake!'

'Sorry.'

'You been there all night?'

'Some of it.'

Guessing rightly that Smiler had shared his time between himself and Aunt May, Mike softened his tone as he sighed and said, 'How is she today?'

'Just the same.'

Mike lay for a moment staring at the ceiling, while Smiler stared at him. 'OK, I'm gonna shower, get things sorted and be off.' He slipped the covers back and got out of bed.

'There's something you should know.'

What the hell now? Mike thought, turning to face him. Why can't he ever just come out with it? For Christ's sake, sometimes it's like pulling friggin' teeth!

'What?' Mike demanded.

'Shelly's gone.'

Mike sat back on the bed. He sighed. It's not as if I wasn't expecting it. Just had a lot more questions for her. Damn. Wish she'd waited around a bit longer.

He looked at Smiler. 'OK- I'm guessing there's more.'

Smiler nodded solemnly. 'There is. The guard on Shelly's door was murdered as well…with a gun.'

'Yeah, that'll do it all right.'

'Shelly attacked the murderer with a pair of metal coat hangers, ripped his eyeball out, and some of his gum.'

Impressed, Mike raised his eyebrows. 'OK, so where's the bastard now?'

'Next door, and Aunt May's in the room on the other side. Somebody figured it would be easier to guard you all if you were together.'

'Wow.'

Feeling like he'd finally done something right, Smiler dropped his head, but Mike saw the smile.

Quickly jumping up from the bed, Mike hastily pulled his jeans on, splashed cold water over his face then, with Smiler in tow, strode out of the room. He paused for a moment at the door. Behind him Smiler, guessing he would want to check the assassin out first, said, 'Right.'

Mike swung to the right. A few quick steps, and he was outside the assassin's room. Nodding at the guard, he stared through the window. Most of the man's face was covered in bandages- at least, the side he could see was. 'Hmm,' he muttered. Turning, he walked along the corridor to Aunt May's room.

'I see the monk's at his usual station. Has he even moved at all?'

Smiler shrugged. 'Where else would he be? Anyhow, he spent as much time praying over you.'

Sighing, Mike pushed the door open. 'Any change?'

Brother David looked up and shook his head. 'How are you?'

'Never better. Bit sore, but it'll heal.'

'Still leaving us?'

'No choice. You know as well as I do someone's got to stop this madness. God only knows where that nutter Mr Leader has set up shop now. How many more kids is he gonna ruin, torture, murder? If I find him, I'll find the main bastards behind this. But first - Tony.'

'That the plan?'

'Got a better one?'

'Why can't you just leave it, Mike? We're all alive, surely that's the main thing.'

'For how fucking long?' Mike snapped. 'You just don't get it, do you? These creeps won't give up until we're all dead, you included. They will wipe out everyone who knows about them. For God's sake, Dave, you lived with them for long enough, you know just how ruthless they are.'

Brother David glanced at Aunt May, then back at Mike. The pain in his eyes tore right into Mike, but it only strengthened his resolve.

'I have to do it, Dave, you know this.'

'I will pray for your soul, brother.'

'Better pray hard,' Smiler quipped.

Mike gave him a look, then turned back to Brother David. 'Well, I suppose it'll be good to know I've got God on my side. Bit of celestial help won't go amiss.'

Ignoring his flippancy, Brother David said, 'Take the boy with you. You'll need him.'

'No way.'

Behind him, Smiler tutted. Shrugging, Mike walked over to Brother David. Squeezing his shoulder, he said, 'Look after them for me- Brother David.'

Brother David smiled. For a moment his heart lifted. He had been waiting a long time for Mike to accept what he was, and had not realised until now just how much it really meant to him. He covered Mike's hand with his, and whispered, 'Take care, Mike.'

Mike nodded. 'I will. And make sure you take care of Aunt May and Smiler.'

Brother David squeezed Mike's hand. When he finally let go, Mike looked at the still form of Aunt May, covered in wires and tubes, all doing for her what she should be doing for herself. He leaned forward and kissed her cheek, her skin was scraped where she'd slid down the wall and Mike gently touched the spot. Then, with a quick glance at Smiler, and a nod at Brother David, he turned and walked out of the room.

Smiler was at his heels as Mike went into the assassin's room. Reaching the bed, Mike grabbed the man's face and twisted it towards him. The man moaned, and his uncovered eye opened. He stared at Mike for a moment then, realising who had his jaw in a death-like grip, his eye filled with fear.

'Right, you bastard. Tell me who put you up to this, or I'll rip your fucking head off.'

Although he had been expecting something along those lines, Smiler still gulped at the sheer ferociousness in Mike's voice, and stepped back.

'Tell me!' Mike shook the man's head as hard as a terrier would shake a rat.

'I…I don't know,' he practically screamed. 'It was a phone call.'

Mike laughed. 'Get many calls like that, do you?'

'A few.'

'Liar, fucking liar… Tell me who owns you. And that's the operative word, isn't it? Truth is, they think of you as highly as they think of us, and we both know how much that is. Wise up, bastard, and tell me, or I swear to God you'll never get out of this room alive. You're nothing but a useless piece of fucking scum that the world will be better off without, you and your friggin' parasite masters, and whoever allies with them. So tell me. Because, trust me, I'll drag it out of you one way or another. Now. Tell me now.' Mike was practically nose to nose with him and screaming in his face.

The shadow that crossed over the man's one good eye told Mike he was close to the bone. 'Fucking tell me!' He shook the man's head again.

But the assassin's eye still said no as he stared defiantly at Mike.

Mike let go of the man's jaw, and transferred his grip to his throat. He squeezed until the muscles stood out on his arm. The man's face grew red, but still he held that stubborn stare.

'No, Mike.' Smiler stepped forward and put his hand on Mike's arm. 'Don't.'

But Mike shook him off. As his grip tightened, the man's face lost the red and took on a purple hue.

'Please, Mike,' Smiler begged, his hand latching back on and tightening around Mike's arm. 'Don't do it… It will make you worse than them.'

Mike squeezed harder. Then, after a moment, Smiler's words seemed to sink in and his grip relaxed slightly. The man sucked in some much-needed air as he struggled to sit up.

Arms folded across his chest, legs planted firmly apart, Mike watched him struggle. When he was fully upright, Mike leaned forward. 'Well?'

'Fuck off,' came the mumbled reply.

'Something original, please.' Using as much force as he could, Mike backhanded him. The man's head swung to the right, the stitches in his mouth burst open and blood spewed from his mouth.

After a minute the man smirked, a cruel sarcastic edge to his mouth. Slowly he shook his head. He massaged his throat with his right hand, ran his left across his mouth, and flicked the blood in Mike's direction. For a brief moment, Smiler almost wished he'd let Mike strangle him.

'Do you honestly think anything you can do would be worse than they can?' he said, spitting out blood.

'Tell me.'

'Have you any idea what they will do if they find out I even told you the fucking time of day?'

'Who's they?'

'Go fuck yourself.'

'Is that the best you can come out with?' Mike raised his fist and slammed it into his mouth.

Spitting out more blood, the man said, 'Doesn't matter. You're marked. Dead man walking. There's plenty looking for you… And as for that bitch,' he spat the last word out with more blood, 'she is going to suffer, believe me. Slowly!'

Guessing that he meant Shelly, Mike grabbed him by the throat. 'Like this, you mean?' Slowly he squeezed again.

Smiler's eyes flicked from one to the other. Leaning over the bed, he begged, 'Just tell him, please, or he'll kill you. Please, mister, tell him what he wants to know.'

For a moment the fear came back to the man's face. Then, as if finally giving up, his whole body slumped against the pillows. 'Either way, I'm as dead as you are. Once they find out I failed. There are no second chances.' Resigned to his fate, he slowly closed his eyes. Unlike Mike, he truly knew the full extent of what he was up against.

Mike looked at Smiler and, with a twitch of his head towards the door, mouthed silently, 'Outside.'

Smiler moved quickly. The look on Mike's face gave him no other options.

Watching Smiler walk past the window, Mike waited until he was certain he was gone before grabbing the thin bed sheet. Quickly, he tore it into strips while the man watched with mounting horror. Mike grabbed the man's hands and tied them in front of him, then stuffed a wad of the sheet into his bleeding mouth and tied it in place with one of the strips before spinning him over onto his stomach. Unbuckling his belt, and using all of his strength, Mike lashed him nine times, making each lash count. Despite the rag in his mouth, the man still managed to moan loudly after each lash. When Mike was finally finished, he flung him onto his back. The man's feet beat a quick tattoo on the bed in a failed attempt to ease the pain.

Mike tore the bloody gag out of his mouth. 'Like that, did

you, eh? Well, that's what the people you work for do to young women, and men, only they don't use a single belt. They use a cat o' nine tails. Each tail rips into their flesh, gouging holes in their bodies. Nine times they do this. Picture it! And you, bastard, aren't even bleeding. I've seen the body of one young women who was so terrified she actually bled to death through the pores in her skin!'

The man blinked. His back was on fire, but through it all he knew he had got off lightly. He started to talk then, and suddenly couldn't stop. In ten minutes Mike found out just about everything he needed to know, and more. He had the feeling that the man had used him to offset his guilt, a chance to buy his way into Dave's heaven.

'Doubt that's ever gonna happen, bastard!' he muttered on his way to the door.

CHAPTER NINETEEN

Shelly stepped down from the cab. Feeling rather foolish, she thanked the driver for the lift. Gotta stop thinking everybody's out to get me! God, all he did was accidentally brush my hand. But then, after all that's happened, especially this last week, no one could blame me for being friggin' paranoid.

'It was my pleasure, love,' the driver said with a smile. 'Hope you get where you're going safely. Take care. Bye now!' He waved as he pulled away.

Shelly nodded and waved back. When he'd gone, she looked around. He'd said that the train station was at the bottom of this narrow back street, so with no time to waste she headed off in that direction. 'Gotta be a bank somewhere near the station,' she muttered.

The street was totally empty, apart from a black mongrel dog pissing up someone's back gate. I feel the same, she thought, as she passed. Who the hell paints their back gate pink?

Knowing she was letting her mind wander to stop herself from going mad, she concentrated on her plan.

She had to draw all of her savings out. She didn't have a lot, but six hundred quid would tide her over for a short time. She knew that it would be traced- that's what she wanted, figuring that they would think she was heading for London, when in reality she was going anywhere but there.

She would buy a ticket to London on her card, then pay cash for a ticket to where she really was heading, hoping against hope that it would put them off the trail. It was a plan, of sorts. Actually, the only plan she had.

At the end of the road, she stepped into a totally different world. Having never visited Manchester before, she was surprised to find a vibrant, busy city with wall to wall people, even this early on a morning. Spotting Oxford Road Station over to her left, she scanned the rest of the road. Nothing suspicious going on, no loiterers. The dog padded past her as if she didn't even exist. Just looks like an ordinary day with ordinary folk going about their business.

Deciding to turn left, she walked on for a few minutes and spotted a bank just opening. OK, she thought, so far so good.

Nearly tripping over a shopping trolley wheeled by an old woman in a red coat, she apologised and hurried into the bank. Even though it was the old woman's fault, Shelly didn't want her making a fuss and drawing attention to them. The small queue quickly evaporated, and Shelly was looking at a bald middle-aged man in short sleeves and a black waistcoat that was far too tight.

After a few minutes, he squinted at her, then at the form she'd handed him, then back at the screen. After he'd done this twice, he shoved the form back through the space in the window and said, 'Sorry, no funds.'

'What? No, you're wrong, there's plenty in there to cover it. Well, enough anyhow. Please try again.'

Shrugging, he tried again, then looked at her and shook his head.

Shelly's heart sank. Plan A buggered before lift off, she thought. Turning away from him, her heart fluttering wildly, she headed for the door.

She held onto her tears, wanting to cry, wanting to scream her frustration to the world. How could she ever have thought that she could outwit them in any way? They were way ahead of her. She knew that every corner she turned would be blocked. The hundred or so quid she had on her wouldn't last long. Feeling pretty desperate, she started thinking she should just give up and let them do whatever they were going to do to her. Better now than after the God knows how many hours of anxiety she had to face.

Feeling a bit shaky, and guessing rightly that her blood sugar was dropping rapidly, she went into the first café she came to and ordered a coffee and a slice of chocolate cake. Half an hour later, after going through numerous mind changes, she finally realised that there really was nothing else she could do but go for it, whatever happened. Better to try, at least, than just friggin' give up and fade away.

If I'm gonna die, might as well go down fighting the bastards!

Her resolve strengthened, she left the coffee shop and headed along the street to a chemist. After buying hair dye and a pair of scissors, she booked into a cheap hotel for the night. She was shown to her room by an old man wearing a blue and red striped hoodie. He huffed and puffed up the two flights of stairs, hauling himself up by the rail. By the time they reached her room, his face was as red as the stripes on his shirt. Taking the key from his outstretched hand, she thanked him. Out of breath, he could only nod in reply. She watched as, without looking back, he began the slow journey down the stairs.

Once inside, she quickly locked the door behind her. Looking round, she was surprised to see the place was reasonably tidy. The pale blue sheets were clean, and the room smelled fresh enough, as if everything had just been polished. The carpet wasn't sticky and looked like it had just been hoovered.

Could have been worse, she thought, moving to the window. Hiding behind the yellow flowered curtain, she moved the cream net covering the window and peeped up and down the street. Heaving a sigh of relief after five minutes of scanning the road in both directions, and seeing no one taking any interest in the hotel, she went into the tiny bathroom. Taking the scissors from her bag, she started to chop her long black hair.

Shelly remembered how she'd wanted to be a hairdresser, and

how she had trained for all of three months before she got well sick of it and decided her true vocation was to be a reporter for a big newspaper.

'That's what got me into this friggin' mess,' she muttered, watching her hair mount up in the sink. She kept on cutting until she had a really short urchin style. Running her fingers through, she spiked it up slightly on top and was pleased with the result.

Tomorrow, when I'm blonde, even the Brothers Grim won't recognise me, she thought, as she watched the last strands of hair swirl and disappear down the plug-hole.

She dyed her hair, and left it on longer than it stated on the box. Going from black to blonde could be tricky. A friend of hers had once woken her up at six in the morning, begging for help because her hair had gone bright green.

A couple of hour later, satisfied with the results of her hair, she was watching the small TV. But her mind couldn't settle. After another of her frequent trips to the window, she again lay down on the bed. Slowly her lids drooped and in moments she was asleep.

CHAPTER TWENTY

Danny Wilson lay sprawled across his settee, last night's untouched TV dinner still lying on the floor next to a cold bowl of tomato soup. He had one hand behind his head and the other holding onto his ribs, which seemed to be getting worse by the hour. After x-rays, they had told him at the hospital that his ribs weren't actually broken, just severely bruised.

'To hell with what they say,' he groaned. Again he wondered just what the hell he'd ever done to deserve everything that had happened over the last few weeks. He gently rubbed his hand over the worst spot. 'The bastards seem fairly broken to me.'

In a semi-doze a few minutes later, he was suddenly wide awake when he heard a heavy banging on the door. 'What the----?' he muttered, struggling to sit up. ' Keep yer fucking hair on, I'm coming,' he yelled, as the banging was repeated over and over.

'For fuck's sake, this better be good.'

He opened the door. It took all of his strength to stop it from banging into him and crushing him against the wall, as Shelly's brothers burst in.

'Ha'way, man!' Danny yelled at the two men. 'What do you think you're doing, yer thick pair of twats?'

'Where is she?' Gary, thickset, and built like a heavyweight boxer, yelled in his face.

'Not you lot again, for fuck's sake,' Danny muttered. For a moment, he was thrown - it was a repeat performance of a few days ago, when the Brothers Grim, as Shelly called them, had just barged in and taken over.

'What did you say?' Gary demanded, while Shelly's other brother, Liam, taller and much thinner, stepped forward, about to try, as usual, to placate him. Gary brushed him off before he had a chance to say anything, and glared at Danny.

'Nothing,' Danny sighed, turning from the door and thinking, no need to ask them in, seeing as the cheeky bastards are already in the flaming house.

Followed by Gary and Liam, who closed the door behind him, Danny hobbled along to the sitting room and eased himself down on to the settee. 'I'm guessing this is about Shelly.'

'Taking the piss, or what? Of course it's about our Shelly. We've been to the hospital, and she's gone walkabout again.'

'Nowt to do with me.'

'Yeah, that's what you said the last time.'

'That's true, and look what sort of fucking mess I ended up in! So forgive me if I say I've fucking well had enough. Piss off, why don't you?'

'We need to know where she is. You know fine well she's a diabetic. She needs her meds.'

'Yeah, well- like I already said, it's nowt to do with me. I for one don't fucking want to know where she is any more. I couldn't care less if I never see her again. And she's got her stuff, I dropped it off last night. Got it? Now get out.'

'If I find out you're lying----'

'Just fucking see yourselves out, will yer?' Refusing to move, Danny stared stubbornly at the fireplace. He didn't even want to give them the time of day. He'd had more than enough, and still had not come to terms with the events of the last week, when a very good friend had been savagely murdered.

He'd been questioned relentlessly by the coppers from hell, more than once. Locked up in a drugs den and forced to work for the sick bastards filling little plastic bags with little yellow pills.

Had the shit kicked out of me.

More than once an' all.

No fucking more.

If Shelly wants to get herself killed, chasing those friggin' loonies, that's up to her.

Gary glared at Danny, while Liam tried to ease him towards the door. 'Come on, you heard him.'

Danny still stared at the fire, oblivious to Shelly's brothers. Where is she now? he thought.

Why the hell couldn't she just stay put in the bloody hospital?

There's a funeral to go to in a few days' time- has she forgotten her best friend is dead, murdered by those bastards?

But that's Shelly all over, selfish to the core. Evan could really do with seeing her.

Not that I want to, ever again.

But in his mind the words didn't quite ring true.

He'd already decided through a sleepless night that yes, he still loved her, even after everything she'd done. But there was nothing he could do to help her, not in the condition he was in. It even hurt to breathe, for Christ's sake.

He heard the front door slam and shuddered. Pulling a blanket over his head, he groaned. It was all he could do to keep the tears away.

CHAPTER TWENTY-ONE

Standing outside the hospital, Mike took in great gulps of air as he tried not to be sick again. He wiped his mouth, tasting the bitterness, and sighed. What he had just done went right against everything he believed in. He was no stranger to violence, having used it on more than one occasion, but only when absolutely necessary - mostly in the defence of himself or others.

He told himself that this time he had done what had to be done. It was more than necessary, there were too many lives at stake. But his conscience niggled at him. The man had been helpless.

'And so is the whole world. No one is safe anywhere,' he muttered angrily, stepping away from the wall and moving off in the direction of the car park. He shook himself, and made a promise not to beat himself up any more. What had to be done, would be done. He had no choice.

Reaching his car, he jumped in and headed for Newcastle city centre. Managing to grab a parking spot in Grey Street, he walked up to the monument. He stood on the steps and looked down at what was once called- by someone he couldn't remember - the best curved street in England. Where had that thought come from? He allowed himself a half smile. Of course, it was linked to Smiler. Wasn't everything these days?

No doubt Smiler would know who he was, and who built the street, and probably the number of bricks it took. How many work-men there were, what they had for their meals and God only knows what friggin' else. He sighed, knowing that he would probably never see any of the others ever again.

Kristina, you've got damn good timing. Guess it's another time, another place, he was thinking, as he turned and headed in a brisk walk towards Pilgrim Street police station.

Twenty minutes later he was back in his car and driving towards Wallsend, with a three-month extended leave. He badly needed some equipment and knew a man who knew another man, both of whom owed him big time. He'd saved their skins a few years ago when, probably for the first time in their seedy little lives, they had been totally innocent of the crime they had been accused of. Mike could have had them both, Quinn and his right hand man, sent down for a long stretch, but it wasn't the way he did things.

After parking the car, the pub he walked into had definitely seen better days. He was surprised, though, to find decorators inside scraping off years of old red and green flock wall paper. Hmm, with so many pubs closing down, these are obviously flourishing, he thought, propping his leg on the brass guard-rail that ran around the bottom of the bar, and resting both elbows on the bar top. He looked around. Three old men sat in the corner playing cards, while a couple of youths in jeans and t-shirts played the fruit machines. Another youth, sitting in the far corner with his hood up, sat staring into his drink.

'Can I help you?' asked the barman, a younger Boy George look alike. With a toss of his head, he looked Mike up and down while he flicked imaginary dust off the bar with his tea towel. Obviously liking what he saw, he smiled and winked.

'Larry Quinn anywhere around?'

'Who wants to know?' he asked, his attitude immediately becoming defensive.

Knowing that Quinn was probably sitting in the office out the back, Mike replied, 'Just tell him an old friend of his is here to see him. Now.'

'He's not in.'

Mike leaned over the bar. 'Get him now,' he snarled. 'If you know what's good for you.'

Boy George stepped back and, with a loud 'Oh!' disappeared through an open door in the middle of the bar.

A few minutes later he flounced back through the doorway. Closing the door behind him, he said with a huge smile, 'I have to have a name, and if he doesn't know you, you're dead.'

'Yeah, we'll see about that. Tell him he ain't getting a name and if he's not out here in one minute, he's fucking dead. And if you aren't careful, you'll be joining him.'

Boy George looked wide-eyed at him for a moment, then pursed his lips and blew Mike a kiss.

Mike reached out and, pretending to grab it, said, 'Want this shoving up your fucking arse, or what? Better yet, I'll shove it up Quinn's arse, eh?'

Boy George let his hands drop to his hips, struck a pose and replied, 'Oh well, I wouldn't do that. Not if I were you.'

'To hell with this.' Mike moved round the bar. Lifting the flap, he said, as he reached the door, 'I'll tell him myself.'

'Ooooh, you can't do that!' By now Boy George was hopping from foot to foot.

'Watch me.'

Mike pushed him out of the way with one hand and pushed the door open with the other, knocking over a stack of glasses in the process.

He heard Boy George gasp in fear. Serves the daft sod right, Mike thought. Who the hell leaves stacks of glasses lying around?

Mike found himself in a short corridor with a door at each end. Knowing the one on the left led to the Gents, he turned to the right. Five steps and he was turning the handle.

Before he could step through the door, Boy George scuttled under his arm and said, his voice more high pitched than ever, 'It wasn't my fault, boss, he pushed his way in, he did honest, I never stood a chance.'

Quinn took one look at Mike and said, in a heavy smoker's voice with a slight hint of Irish, 'It's all right. Get out.' He reached over to the radio and cut off Dolly Parton in the middle of Nine Till Five. Nearly tripping over himself in his haste, Boy George got out.

Of medium build, Quinn had black hair and vivid blue eyes, eyes that were deceiving, eyes that were warm at first but could cut you down in seconds. His nose was flattened across his pock marked face, a remnant from his fighting days. Fighting was where Quinn had made his name, a name that struck fear into the hearts of many people - especially those who owed him money.

Looking at Mike, those eyes were calm. Mike had saved his skin, and so he was family.

'I'm guessing this is not a social call. What I can do for you? Just name it.'

One thing about Quinn, Mike thought, he didn't beat about the bush. That was the only thing Mike liked about him. If he'd known any other way to get what he wanted, he would have taken it rather than be standing here.

'I want a gun.' He hesitated for a moment, then went on, 'No. Make that two.'

Quinn didn't even raise his eyebrows. 'OK, what sort? Hand guns, machine gun?'

'Actually, make that three. Two handguns, one machine. And

throw in a couple of knives for good measure. And plenty ammo.'

This did make Quinn raise his eyebrows. 'You taking on the world, or what?'

'Something like that.'

'How about a couple of grenades while we're at it?' Quinn asked, only half joking.

Mike shrugged. Might come in handy, he thought. 'Sure. Why not.'

Quinn studied Mike for a moment. 'If you need help, you only have to say the word.'

'No, thank you.'

'OK, but the offer will stand for as long as you need it. Just give me a call. If you tell me the problem, you never know - I might be able to make it go away.'

Mike shook his head. 'Doubt it.'

Seeing that he wasn't going to get any more information, Quinn shrugged and picked up the phone. 'How soon?'

'Now.'

'A miracle worker I'm not.'

Saying nothing, Mike stared him out.

Quinn spoke into the phone. 'How soon can you get them here?' He listened for a moment, before turning to Mike. 'An hour, hour and a half?'

'OK, guess that'll have to do. How much?'

'On the house.'

Not wanting to be beholden to Quinn for anything, Mike was adamant. 'No way.'

'I insist. That's the only way the deal will go down.'

Mike ground his teeth. He was desperate, and Quinn knew it. 'Right, I'll be back in an hour or so. And I was never here, understand?'

'Of course that goes without saying.'

'Just so that you know.' Mike stared at him for a moment, then spun round and walked out the door.

CHAPTER TWENTY-TWO

Deciding to pop over to Durham, Mike jumped into his car. He needed to sort things out with his neighbours regarding his flat, and grab some clothes. Then he would head south as soon as he'd picked up the guns from Wallsend.

He was thinking of Shelly, and what she had told him. It was starting to make more sense every time he thought of it. He wondered how many people had been murdered down the ages, just to keep the secret. And how deep into it all was Tony?

No way could he be in with them!

And if he was, how had he become involved? Tony, for all intents and purposes, was his brother - maybe not by blood, but by an even stronger bond. I know him inside out, it's not his style to become involved with the bad guys. Has he somehow become indebted to them? If so, how? Why?

One thing though, that Shelly sure is one plucky kid. She made mincemeat outta that ugly fellow all right. Hope she's safe, wherever she might be.

The drive took just under thirty minutes. Some days it could take over an hour or more. Using the Tyne Tunnel wouldn't help, not at the moment anyhow, as they were building a long-awaited new one, and everything was down to one lane.

He pulled into the bottom of his street. Guess I've been lucky, he thought. God knows how long it'll take to get back when the kids are out of school.

Am I in a hurry?

Well, whichever poor bastard is about to die at the hands of whatever fiend our lords and masters have dispatched, I guess they would say a very loud yes!

He'd had to park a few doors down the street from his flat, as the street was wall to wall cars. On a fine day in Durham, you grabbed a space where you could, unless you wanted to pay a fortune in car parking fees.

He'd tell the couple in the flat below that he'd be away for a few months, ask them to take the mail in, generally keep an eye on things. Not that there was ever any bother in this neck of the woods. Nice and quiet. Just how he liked it.

And they wouldn't take much asking, he thought with a wry smile as he locked the car. Gav would love the job of guardian. He was without doubt the nosiest person in the street- perhaps even the whole of the flaming North- and he was seconded only, by his lovely wife April.

He knocked on their door before going up to his flat. He frowned when there was no answer, and knocked again.

Strange, he thought. Gavin and April, in their fifties and both riddled with arthritis, hardly ever went out. In fact, on a warm day Gav was usually sat out in his wheel chair at the door on gossip alert. Shrugging, he moved to the window. Cupping his hands at the sides of his face to block the sun, he peered inside.

At first he could barely make anything out. Then what was in front of him began to make sense.

Stepping back, he gasped, the image flickering in his mind like some old black and white film. April and Gav, both naked, lay side by side on the floor, their twisted arthritic legs spread awkwardly. Both had been scourged. Ribbons of flesh were flung every which way, one ribbon intertwined in their clasped hands.

CHAPTER TWENTY-THREE

The short, muscular man camouflaged in brown trousers, dark green jacket and cap, had Mike in his sights. He'd known that his quarry would have to turn up here eventually. He'd actually turned up sooner than the man had expected. The trees the man was hiding in, across the street from the neat row of whitewashed houses, were perfect cover. Really, he thought, with a certain glee, I couldn't have picked a better place for a kill.

His finger was ready to squeeze the trigger, the pressure slowly mounting, when an old woman in a red coat, bright yellow hat, and long strands of dirty grey hair hanging around her shoulders - walked in front of him.

For fuck's sake! he thought, raising the gun skywards. Get out of the friggin' way, you stupid old cow!

But she stumbled, rolling from side to side like some small, brightly painted fishing boat on a rough sea.

'Fucking move,' he muttered, his frustration mounting. He never liked to make a secondary killing, it left far too many loose ends. Everything kept neat and tidy, that was his motto, always had been, always would be.

That's the way of it.

In the circles he moved in, he was well known for his tidiness. Tidy was what his punters liked. No loose ends. Nothing to tie either him or them to the kill. Satisfaction doubly guaranteed-then on to the next one.

They had trained him well from birth, his masters, though he'd never met any of them face to face. From what he'd been told by others in the trade, that was the best way.

On the island where he'd grown up, he'd speculated once or twice on who they really were. A few whispered questions, and the answers he'd received had been more than enough to make him keep his head down and his mouth shut.

Oblivious to what was taking place just yards from him, and the possibility that he was only moments from death, Mike was leaning against the wall, staring at the old woman but barely seeing her, because of the tears in his eyes.

April and Gav, dead because of me. Two of the nicest people in the world!

Why?

A warning!

To stop. Before I even start.

How many more?

He blinked, and the tears dried. What the hell to do?

At that moment, filled with despair, he felt like giving up. Running off somewhere, hiding, getting a new identity, letting the world and everyone in it take care of themselves.

What can I do against scum that seem to know every move I make? Bastards!

'No,' he muttered. 'Can't just walk away from this.'

But no way can I report what's happened here, it'll keep me tied up for days. Give the bastards more time to bring others down, as well as me.

Who the fuck's next?

Surely somebody in the street's gotta be wondering where April and Gav are, for God's sake. Surprised it hasn't been reported already. Someone must be wondering why Gav isn't on his perch by the door.

Unless it's just happened - which means the hit man could still be hanging around.

For a second, his heart leaped. No, the bodies look like they've been there at least a day or two. It probably happened right in the middle of their daytime TV.

He looked at the old woman in the bright clothes across the street. She's drunk. He smiled briefly, but it was an automatic smile. Superimposed on his view of the woman was the memory of the flies buzzing around his neighbours' bodies.

I'll phone it in from a phone box, anonymously. That way they won't be able to link me in.

Shit! They'll know I've been working on similar cases.

Oh, Jesus!

Mike sighed. The road just kept on getting steeper every corner he turned.

The assassin never felt the bullet enter the side of his neck. It was over in seconds. The bullet exploded in his windpipe, a neat kill by someone who was as meticulous as he was. His body crumpled slowly as he took his last breath, and hit the soft soil with a low thud, heard only by the old woman in the red coat. With a twitch of her lips in recognition of a job well done, she straightened up and went on her way.

At the top of the street, she was met by a young blonde woman. They spoke for a few minutes before a car, driven by a woman with a brown ponytail, pulled up and they both got in. The old woman sat in the back. She pulled off the yellow bullet-proof hat and straggly grey wig to reveal a much younger woman, a stunning brunette. She shook her hair loose as she shrugged out of the shapeless padded coat, which revealed her bullet-proof vest.

'Well done, Louise,' said the pony-tailed driver to the blonde woman in the front seat.

Very pleased that everything had gone according to plan, Louise nodded. 'And you, Coral,' she said over her shoulder.

'We've been after that one for a good while. They'll be well pleased back home.' Coral's voice had a soft Scottish burr. She grinned as she rubbed her hands in satisfaction. 'The world's a wee bit safer place now.'

The two in the front nodded. The driver, Ella, grinned at Coral. 'You can say that again. But please don't.'

Unaware of the drama unfolding mere yards from him, Mike hurried down to his car. Once behind the wheel he took the road back to Wallsend, planning to phone the murders of April and Gav into the nearest station from there. After that, he was on his way. Nothing was going to stop him!

These freaks might think they're above the law. But they are about to find out they ain't above mine!

CHAPTER TWENTY-FOUR

Brother David was staring at Smiler, and had been for quite a while. Smiler hadn't moved in the last hour. After a sudden outburst of what sounded like pure gibberish, and repeatedly counting his fingers, he had been sitting ramrod straight and staring out the window.

Brother David sighed, knowing no way to help ease this child's obviously tormented soul, and only guessing at the reasons for his neurotic behaviour. He could only pray for him. He clasped his hands together and bowed his head.

'What the bloody----?'

Brother David's eyes shot open. As if someone had suddenly flipped a switch, Smiler spun round. Both of them stared in awe as Aunt May struggled to sit up.

'Don't just bloody sit there, give me a hand,' she demanded, glaring at them.

As Brother David jumped up to help her, Smiler hurried round to the other side of the bed and plumped her pillows up.

'Thank you, Smiler.'

Easing back and resting her head, she looked at each of them in turn. 'OK, who's gonna fill me in here? And why have I got such a bloody headache?'

Five minutes later, the tale as they knew it told, Brother David rose. 'I'll pop along and get the nurse.'

'Do you have to be such a bloody tittle tattle? Really, I'm fine, and ready for home. Just get my clothes and we can get out of here.' She looked accusingly at Brother David. 'You know I can't stand hospitals. Horrible bloody places.'

Smiler looked at her wide-eyed. As ignoring her Brother David left to find a nurse. 'Jesus, Aunt May.' Smiler gasped. 'You can't go home yet, you've just woken up out of a coma!'

'The plants need watering.'

'I'll do it.'

'There'll be guests to sort.'

'All sorted.'

'Dishes washed?'

'Done.'

'Clever bugger!'

'Bloody hell!' she said a moment later, 'what about the Shetland pony?' Shetland pony was Aunt May's name for the huge dog, Tiny, who Mike had rescued from an empty flat in London.

'Jill and her girls are looking after Tiny. So, see, there's nothing to worry about.'

She looked down at her hands for a brief moment, then back

at Smiler. 'Where are the other two?' she asked in a quiet voice, with an unspoken, they should be here.

Smiler was quick to Mike's defence. 'Mike's had to go. Honestly, he's just gone, really, but he's been here all of the time with me, and Brother David. Don't know about Tony, though. No one can get in touch with him.' Smiler shrugged. 'Mike won't tell us everything either, he says we're in danger if we know it all… Er, do you know who clobbered you?'

She shook her head, and winced slightly.

'Please be careful.' Smiler gently patted her hand.

Aunt May placed her other hand on top of Smiler's, sandwiching his between hers. 'You are a good, kind, caring boy, Smiler.'

Smiler felt the blood rush to his face. She's talking about me! he thought in amazement.

'Yes, I mean you, son,' she said, as if she'd read his mind.

Smiler's mind was in a whirl. Oh God! She doesn't know the things I've done.

She thinks I'm nice.

I'm not.

I've done terrible things, really bad disgusting things just to get drugs and food.

I'm not the person she thinks I am!

He hung his head, his heart breaking. She'll hate me, really hate me when she knows what I've done.

He looked at the scars on his arm, and for a moment wanted to feel the sharp knife in his hand, feel the release as the blood ran freely and dripped to the floor.

Sensing the turmoil going on inside him, Aunt May squeezed his hand to reinforce what she had just said.

Still staring at his arms, he shook his head. She's going to hate me. When she finds out, she'll look at me with disgust. I couldn't bear that, to see it on her face.

'Look at me, Smiler.'

After a moment, he lifted his head and looked into her eyes. She smiled. 'You're with family now. What's past is past. You have a future with us.'

His breath caught in his throat, and his heart swelled with emotions he couldn't ever remember feeling before. Could this truly be so? Could life actually be worth living, instead of just drifting from day to day?

Just then the doctor, arrived, trailing a couple of nurses and Brother David. He was a young, fair-haired man, who chose every opportunity he could to flash his perfect white teeth. Aunt May found herself staring at those teeth. She found the smile that went with them predatory.

For God's sake, get me outta this bloody place, she was thinking, as the doctor moved closer.

'Well,' he said, flashing his teeth again. 'You've given us quite a scare. We weren't sure if you would make it or not, a head wound at your age.' He shook his head as if talking down to a child, raising Aunt May's blood pressure to a dangerous level.

'But look at you. I dare say you're on the mend already, yes?' He grinned at her.

Prat! Aunt May was thinking, but said, 'Yes, well, I'm fine now, doctor. I just want to go home, thank you very much.'

'Can't let you do that, I'm afraid. We need to do more tests.'

'Why? I'm perfectly all right, young man.'

She's probably as stubborn as Mike, Smiler thought, remembering Mike's determination to go home.

'Aunt May.' Brother David had moved to her side and rested his hand on her shoulder. 'Please, it's for your own good, and our peace of mind. We need to know that you're truly well enough before we take you home. I'm sure the tests won't take too long.'

Smiler nodded his agreement, willing her to stay for the tests.

Exhausted, she lay back on the pillows. 'OK, OK.' She frowned at the doctor. 'But I'm home as soon as you're finished with me, and I would like that to be some time today, thank you very much. Also, I would like you to remember when you speak to me that I'm not a bloody kid, and I have all my faculties intact!'

'Well,' he practically snapped at her, 'I am sorry if I've offended you in any way.'

'Oh, you have!'

'Again, I apologise'- although the apology came from behind his gritted white teeth.

'Accepted. Now, could you please just bloody well get on with it? Thank you very much.'

'Of course. Well- a lot depends on what we find. Now, if you gentlemen would leave us for a few minutes? We won't be long, but we need to take some blood and check her blood pressure, among other things.' He flashed a smile at Brother David and Smiler.

'No way,' Aunt May stated, folding her arms across her chest. 'They go, I go.'

'I beg your pardon?'

'What for?'

'Well,' he blustered.

'Look, Doc, here's the score. These guys are staying. It's not safe in this dump.'

Brother David's face was pink as he stared at the walls, but he couldn't help thinking that she had a point.

CHAPTER TWENTY-FIVE

The journey back to Wallsend only took ten minutes longer than the one to Durham. Having been driven off a cliff, shot at, and knowing that they would try anything, probably when he was least expecting it, Mike had checked his mirrors constantly as he'd woven in and out of the traffic. He knew he had to be vigilant, because they were probably becoming pretty desperate now, and more than ever determined to finish him off. He'd had a moment or two thinking a red sports car was tailing him, but after ten minutes it took a slip road, and nothing dropped in behind him for the rest of the drive back to Wallsend.

Now at last he was parked outside Quinn's pub. He waited a few minutes, watching everything and everybody that came and went in the street, dissecting every snippet of conversation he managed to catch through the open window. Finally, satisfied that he had not been followed, he got out of the car and went inside.

Spotting him immediately, the Boy George look-alike lifted the flap in the bar top and, with a huge smile on his face, ushered Mike behind the bar. Smile still in place, Boy George ran along the corridor and, after a quick one-two knock, flung the door open.

'He's back, boss,' he trilled as, practically bowing, he stepped aside to let Mike in.

Shaking his head and hiding a grin, Mike walked in, noticing at once the large navy blue holdall on the desk.

'It's here,' Quinn said, tapping the bag with his right forefinger. 'Everything you asked for.'

'How much?' Mike asked, striding over to the desk and picking up the holdall. By the weight of it, he guessed that it did hold everything he wanted. He slung the holdall over his left shoulder.

'On the house.'

'No. I'll pay.'

'No, you won't. I already said. Look, Yorke, you're the straightest copper I ever met. Don't know what the fuck's going on here, but it's obviously something big. If you need any more help, you just have to ask- no strings attached.'

'Thank you.'

'No bother. It feels good to be on the side of the angels for once.' He grinned at Mike.

Unsmiling Mike stared back. Quinn's blue eyes looked genuine enough, and Mike guessed that he would probably be a good ally in what was to come. But did he really want to become what would amount to Quinn's friend? Basically, the man was nothing more than a piece of shit, with no morals at all. Well, perhaps one - and that was the main reason why Mike had gone to bat for him when he'd been accused of running a paedophile ring. Quinn was many things, but a paedophile? No.

Rumour had it that Quinn had personally seen off more than one child molester in his time. And good for him if the rumours are true, and Mike suspected that they were.

But now he has a hold over me!

Mike gritted his teeth. 'I'll bear that in mind.' He turned and walked out.

PART THREE

CHAPTER TWENTY-FIVE

24 hours later

In the small room in the three-star hotel, the Leader sat in a brown wicker chair, his back to the window, his face in shadow and his eyes staring at a stain on the carpet. He raised his head. He glared at the two henchmen for a moment, making them both feel even more uncomfortable than they already were.

'So, when will the new place be ready?' It was a demand more than a question.

The Chinese guard replied, 'Another few days at the most, my Leader.'

'Another few days. I have to live in this, this,' he gestured, taking in the whole room, 'this filthy hovel for a few more days?' His tone was one of shock, his face even more so, as he stood up and spat at the stain on the carpet. 'Are you out of your fucking tiny minds?'

'Maybe a little less, my Leader. They will be as quick as they can. The English guard said quickly, thinking, It's not that bad, for

God's sake, quite luxurious to the way some people have to live. But that's these guys all over. No way could we have put him in a five-star in case he was recognised by a member of the Families, or one of their many servants.

'We have a lot of people working on it, my Leader,' the Chinese guard said into the sudden silence. 'Trust me. Everything will be back to normal before you know it.'

The other guard quickly nodded.

The Leader jumped up from his seat and began pacing the small room. Like the guards, he was dressed in a grey suit and tie instead of his usual monk's habit. His hair had been cut short and brushed back off his forehead with no parting. He was also clean shaven, his ten year old beard gone now. Only someone who had been up close and personal would recognise him.

'We are losing money rapidly, and the longer we wait to get established, the more money we lose. Don't you fucking under-stand simple maths?' He glared at the English guard.

'We'll make it up, my Leader. The drones are on the streets now picking up new workers, just as easily as they did up north, and the chemist has his lab sorted. Production should restart by the end of the week.'

'Not good enough,' the Leader snapped. He knew now that all family money was denied to him. He was truly an outcast. For the moment, war had been declared. It was the way. For now, he was fair game. If he made it to the meeting, then by law he would have his final say.

And I will. I am by the rules allowed to state my case. They can't change that overnight, not without the full consent of every living Family member. For God's sake, they can't get rid of me just for living as we always used to. And they can't shut me up, either.

Fools, the whole bloody lot of them.

Well, they won't use me as a scapegoat, put my life on the line just because things aren't going to plan.

And they know which way I'll vote. They even tried to deny me that!

'How dare they!' he yelled.

He slammed his fist down on the coffee table. Behind him, both guards jumped. It was an automatic reaction in the presence of this man. Every day was a knife-edge existence.

'You realise,' he shouted again, 'that I'll also have to sort some new links for the slaves, if those fools get their own way, and I'm made an outcast for ever?' They both nodded.

The English guard was thinking, That won't be too hard, not with the demand for slaves growing more and more with every passing year.

Then, changing tack altogether, the Leader looked each of the guards up and down, and went on in a totally different tone, 'Any of these new peasants worthy of my attention?'

'Yes, my Leader. Certainly, my Leader, but- is the risk really worth it?' the Chinese guard put in. 'I mean…' The words stumbled in his mouth, frightened of going too far because no one was safe around the Leader. No matter how valuable you thought you were to him, he could snap at any moment. No one was irreplaceable. 'I mean, what if you were recognised, or they gave a description to the police?'

The Leader transferred his gaze to him, and said in wonder, 'Whoever gave you an opinion?'

The guard hung his head. Knowing he'd stepped over the line, he bit his lip as he stared at the floor. But he also knew, if the Leader went down, they would go down with him. That's why they had him in this quiet little hotel, a businessman passing through. Just an ordinary guy. Though in truth, the Leader would stand out in any crowd - they just hoped he wouldn't be recognised for who he was.

They took him out every day as if he was going to work, and drove round and round, anything to entertain him, which was not that easy. Out in the open, they had to be careful of which pastimes they indulged in.

'How about we take you up to the house, see for yourself how the work is progressing?' the English guard said quickly, hoping to divert the Leader's attention from his partner. Sometimes it worked, sometimes it didn't. If not, then you were dead in minutes. One order, and your best friend would kill you. He'd done it himself, more than once, just on the whim of the Leader. He glanced over at his partner, whose skin had turned grey.

A moment later, he sighed with relief as the Leader jumped up and headed for the door. 'Come on,' he said, without looking back. 'What are you waiting for?'

Five minutes later, they were in the car and heading out into the Norfolk countryside.

The journey took twenty-five minutes. The Leader constantly tapped his fingernails on the metal door handle. Both guards were ready to slit their own throats when they finally got there. Jumping out, the Chinese guard quickly opened the door for the Leader. Stepping out of the car, the Leader stared at the huge house. After a moment, he gave a nod of satisfaction. The whole estate was circled by woods, and could not be seen from outside. Like a lot of Family property, If you didn't already know it was here then you never would.

He looked at the workmen moving in and out of the house. Satisfied that they were working hard enough, he said, 'It will do, I suppose. And the back of the property, how big are the grounds? Are they landscaped, do they have the sheds ready?'

'Pretty much the same as the monastery, my Leader,' the Chinese guard replied.

'Hmm.' He strutted back and forth, his mouth set in an arrogant line. 'Not bad, not bad at all.'

'And yes,' the English guard added quickly, 'a couple of more sheds than the monastery had, as you ordered, My Leader. More sheds, more productivity.'

'Good.'

Both guards breathed a silent sigh of relief as they followed him up the broad steps into the house. Inside, it was pretty much a carbon copy of the monastery near Holy Island, just as the leader had demanded.

With a smile, he turned to the guards. 'I think we can move in today, don't you?'

'But your rooms aren't quite ready, my Leader.'

'Then have them ready by tonight. I am not spending another night in that shambles of a hotel. Got it?' Without waiting for an answer, he strode out to the car.

The English guard looked at his partner. 'You stay here and sort it, I'll try to keep him away from here as long as I can.'

'OK. Be careful.'

The English guard nodded before hurrying after the Leader.

CHAPTER TWENTY-SEVEN

Cox knocked on Mr Brodzinski's door. He knew it would take a while for the old man to shuffle along the passageway. He stood here waiting for a good five minutes every Thursday night, when he picked him up for their chess club. He'd been taking the old man for best part of a year now, and actually enjoyed his company. A teller of interesting tales, Mr Brodzinski was, with a storyteller's gift.

The old man peered through the tiny glass spy hole in the door. His stooped body was deceiving- he was still a very strong man. Cox had felt that strength, it was in the shake of his hand among other things. No one knew his first name. He was simply known at the chess club as Brod.

Opening the door, he said, 'Ah, Jason, come in, come in. You have news of my granddaughter?'

Cox's heart sank at the look of hope in Mr Brodzinski's eyes. How the hell am I going to tell him?, he wondered.

'Why don't you go and put the kettle on, Brod? A cup of coffee, please.' He stepped into the house.

Mr Brodzinski nodded. 'And chocolate biscuits?'

'Yes, please.' Cox smiled.

Turning, Mr Brodzinski moved slowly back along the hallway into the kitchen. Urging Cox to sit down at the table, he put the kettle on the gas cooker before switching the small television off. 'Don't know why I listen to the news, it's all bad.' He looked out of the corner of his eye at Cox who, trying to get right in his head what he was going to tell him, was staring at the mix of brightly coloured pansies on the windowsill.

Mr Brodzinski poured boiling water into the teapot for himself, then stirred Cox's coffee. Sitting down opposite him, Mr Brodzinski said, 'So, Jason. I can tell by your face and your silence that there is no news.'

For a moment, Cox breathed in the aroma of his coffee, then said quietly, 'Sorry, Brod. There is some news. Just not the sort of news you want to hear.'

'Please, don't dress it up. If she's dead, just tell me.' He looked at Cox. 'Because if you tell me a lie, it would be so unkind.' With trembling hands, he poured his tea, putting in two sugars and pushing the bowl over to Cox.

Cox stirred his coffee, dropped the spoon on the saucer and looked at Mr Brodzinski. 'OK. I'm sorry for being so blunt, but we can't say for sure if she's alive or dead. From what we've found out, she was definitely in the monastery -apparently a couple of the kids do remember your Annya- but most of their memories of their time in the monastery are a bit fuddled, to say the least.'

Mr Brodzinski frowned. 'Fuddled? What do you mean, "fud-dled"? Is it a word? What sort of word?'

'Mixed up, Brod. It means mixed up.'

'Then say "mixed up"! Honestly, Cox, I'm sure you make words up as you go along.'

Cox sighed. 'They... I'm sorry to tell you this, but they----well. they were all of them controlled by drugs.'

Mr Brodzinski gasped. 'You mean, my Annya…my sweet, beautiful granddaughter...is a drug addict?' His jaw hung open for a moment as he shook his head in disbelief. 'No…no. You have it wrong. It's the wrong girl. It must be… My Annya… No.'

'Through no fault of her own, Brod,' Cox added hastily. 'They were force-fed them.'

'My Annya is a good girl. Just like her mother. She would never take drugs. You have the wrong girl.'

'I'm really sorry, but it was definitely Annya. Her name was also on the list.'

'What list?'

Cox sighed. Already he had said more than he should. He looked his friend in the eye for a moment. What the hell, Brod deserves to know. I know he'll keep his mouth shut.

'What list?' Mr Brodzinski urged him on.

'A list was posted to the station this morning. We don't know who the sender was- no DNA to be found, on the list or the envelope. All we know is that it was posted in London. Although,' he shrugged, 'that could mean anything. It could have been posted there, or anywhere, to throw us off the scent----'

'What sort of list, Jason?' Mr Brodzinski interrupted impatiently. 'You are making it all sound so weird. Why would my Annya's name be on a list?'

'Now that we don't know.' He didn't add that it looked more like a stock list than anything else, as if someone was keeping control of the movements of sheep or cattle. 'The list goes back for more years than you need to know, a list of the names of abducted people, most of them teenagers. So far we've traced people back to the 50s, and we still have a lot more to do. Annya's name is on that list.'

Mr Brodzinski took a moment to digest what Cox had said, then asked, 'So, where is she now?'

Cox sighed. 'I really don't know, Brod. I wish I did.'

'So what is the point of the list? Tell me, why would someone want to send you a pointless list?'

I'm sorry, we don't know that either. The list is only of names, not where they are, or where they were taken from.' He hurried on, hoping Brod hadn't spotted another lie. The list did say where the people had been taken from- but not where they were now.

'What is the point of the list?' Mr Brodzinski grumbled, more to himself than to Cox, as he took a sip of his tea. His shrewd eyes never left Cox's face.

Cox hesitated. They had already gone through that at the station, and the current theory was that somewhere there must be a second, current list, and whoever had sent the first was either playing with them, or seeking revenge.

He quickly went on, 'But the few who remember your granddaughter say she was taken away from the monastery five or six weeks ago, along with four or five other kids.'

'I don't understand. Taken away? Taken to where? And why, why do this to young people?'

'If I knew---- Trust me, if I knew where they were, I would have her home now, along with the rest of them.'

'But who has taken her? Surely you have names of these bad men, if it's been going on that long?'

Perplexed, the old man sat back in his seat. After a moment, he took another drink of his tea. Putting the cup down, he went on, 'Evil men have my granddaughter, don't they?'

'I'm sorry, Brod, but it looks that way. We are doing everything we can, and trust me, we were shocked when we got the list. It was the last thing we expected. For one thing, all of this is on a far bigger scale than we ever thought. But all we have are questions, and no answers.'

Cox was not prepared for the old man banging his walking stick on the table, and actually jumped when all the crockery began to dance. Cups rattled in their saucers, and Cox grabbed for them just before they tipped over.

'I am not stupid! I know the ways of the world. There is more than drugs involved here. They have sold my Annya to even more evil men, and I will never see her again.' A tear ran down his old wrinkled face and dropped on the table.

Cox hadn't wanted to say what they suspected at the station had happened to Annya, and, from what they could gather, many more young people. He reached out and put his hand on Mr Brodzinski's arm. 'Trust me, we won't let it go… I shouldn't tell you this, but a very brave friend of mine is on their tail. I know he won't give up until he finds the ones responsible. And the missing kids. Trust me, he'll bring them home even if he has to walk each and everyone of them the full length and breadth of England!'

He didn't say what he was thinking, that Mike had a better chance working on his own of finding the kids and whoever was behind the scenes than the police had. His suspicions had been aroused by the little that Mike had told him and, doing some discreet digging on his own, he'd been shocked to see how much information had been blocked from above. Katrina was also working on it, and had passed a couple of files over that he had to go through today, before they met up tonight to talk things over.

'Perhaps your man may be able to do this. But can you tell me this, will he find my Annya? And if he does, will she still be the same happy girl she used to be? I think not, Jason. Her life is now ruined. Her life as she knew it, as I knew it…is over.'

PART FOUR

CHAPTER TWENTY-EIGHT

Lovilla Tarasov rested her right hand on a velvet cushion and watched as a young peasant girl painted her nails the same vibrant red as the cushion.

The young blonde girl had been taken from Northumbria. She was Polish by nationality, and had once answered to the name of Annya. Now she was addressed only as 'Hey, you', or 'Peasant' -if she was lucky. She was clearly terrified in case she did something wrong- or, worse, in case the dreaded Lovilla took a fancy to her, as she had to some of the others.

Lovilla had other things on her mind. There was her coming trip to London, where she would be initiated into full Family membership. But what thrilled her more than this was her secret meeting with Count Rene the day after. It was far from their first meeting, and unknown to her father. He would have a fit if he even dreamed of it.

He expects my support? What a shock he's in for, she thought, smiling to herself and putting Annya even more on edge.

As Lovilla held her hands out and examined her nails, Annya

stood next to her, her heart beating so loud she thought the world could hear it.

'Hmm. Quite good,' Lovilla said.

Annya relaxed her fists, only to tighten them again a minute later when Lovilla said, 'You have five minutes to pack, peasant. I will need a slave in London. Move it!'

Annya ran to the room she shared with half a dozen other girls, all used for various jobs around the large house, from cleaning to being a foot warmer on the coldest nights. All the girls were busy elsewhere as Annya threw the few items of clothing she possessed- a thick green jumper that looked like it had once belonged to someone's great grandmother, a pair of wide bottomed jeans that had probably seen the light of day in the sixties, and some underwear- into the holdall they shared for such trips out.

She heard the door open behind her, and fear burning in her heart in case Lovilla had followed her, she spun round. Breathing a sigh of relief, she saw Jaz standing there holding two coat hangers full of assorted clothes.

'You're to try these on and take what fits you, enough for a week. Lucky bitch. It looks like you're going somewhere warm.' Jaz, her auburn bob swishing about her face as she threw the clothes onto Annya's bunk, pulled a face, sighed and went on, 'Please tell me you're gonna try to do a runner?'

Annya nodded, slowly but positively. She was heading home whichever way, and no one was going to stop her. She would die trying. Death was preferable to this living hell.

Annya had been here four or five weeks. She wasn't quite sure which, as the days blurred into one. She knew a couple of them had been spent in a small cell going cold turkey. As Jaz had told her, no one was controlled by drugs here. There was no need to waste them on peasants, there was nowhere to run but out into the snow. Annya had worn only a thin blue shift, the same attire as the others, of which there was a never-ending supply. The house was kept at an even temperature night and day.

Every now and then an arctic blast would skip through the house. Everyone knew that meant someone had been stripped naked and tossed out into the freezing cold. On nights like that, they huddled together praying for their lost friend, and wondering who would be next. In her darkest moments, the only thing that had kept Annya going was that one day, hopefully soon while she was still strong enough, her chance for freedom would come. And when it did, she would be ready.

This was her dream. It was what kept her strong when the sound of the helicopter landing sent waves of fear through them all, when, night after horrendous night, there were guests in the house, and life was even worse than before.

She stared at Jaz. She'd never dreamed her chance would come this soon. She gave a determined nod, and Jaz smiled, her first real smile for a long time. Now the rest of them could dream-dream that Annya would make it.

Jaz had lost three years of her life in this hellhole. She knew that Annya was not the first to attempt an escape. At least two others had done so, but they had never come back, and there had been no rescue. She could only assume they were dead. Tracey had been taken out six months ago and had returned safely, but admitted as she'd cried that she'd been too frightened to try to run. Now all their hopes were pinned on Annya, who she knew was made of much sterner stuff than Tracey.

'Don't let us down, girl,' she whispered as she helped Annya to pack. 'We're all depending on you.'

CHAPTER TWENTY-NINE

After a restless night, tossing and turning between anxiety attacks, Shelly was very surprised to enjoy her breakfast. Though food had been the last thing on her mind as she'd dressed, the rising smell of bacon cooking had lured her downstairs.

She ignored the strange looks from the old man, as she asked for more toast, might as well set myself up for the day she thought , she could see he was dying to ask her if, yesterday, her hair had been long and black and feeling no inclination to put him out of his misery, she smiled as she buttered her toast.

She'd toyed with the idea, on and off through out the night, between her wide awake nightmares, of sending her brothers and Danny a postcard. They would be worrying about where she was. Well, she knew her brothers would - she was hoping that Danny would be, too. Hoping that eventually things would come right between them. But, frightened in case the postcards fell into the wrong hands, she'd decided not to.

Best stay on my own, she'd thought as she counted out the cash for the bill, and thanked the old man for a delicious breakfast, before heading for the train station.

After criss-crossing most of the midlands, by thumb and by train, and one foray further south, using only hard cash, Shelley was certain that she had not been followed. She knew she would be dead by now if she had.

Now, though, she had to find the Leader. She was certain that he was in this part of the country, but where exactly was another matter. Could be this city, or it could be a village around here that no outsider had ever heard of. But she knew without doubt it was somewhere in this area.

Giving the crowds around her a quick once over, she stepped down from the train. In moments, she was swallowed by the sheer mass of moving people. Nipping into the ladies' toilet, she hurried into the first empty cubicle and injected her insulin. That done, she moved to the sink and splashed cold water over her face. She stared into the mirror, still unused to the short blonde crop. She looked from side to side.

It's OK, she thought. Definitely different, anyhow.

Back outside, she grabbed a carton of orange juice and a chocolate biscuit from the cafe. Not what her doctor would recommend at all, but it would keep her sugar levels up and help keep her going until the next proper meal.

Now the hunt begins, she thought. Her plan was to find the lowlifes in the city. No matter how nice the place, or where it was, there were always people who, mostly through no fault of their own, had slipped through the cracks and were living on the edge. It was mostly these young ones that the Families targeted, and leached from society for their own uses, so it was where they hung out that she would get her first lead.

Outside the station, she looked around once more. It was the first time Shelly had been to Norwich, and she was surprised at the mix of lovely old buildings and impressive new ones. Danny would love this place, she thought, with the usual sinking feeling in her heart every time she thought of him.

'Wonder what he's doing now?' she muttered, leaving the station and crossing the road.

CHAPTER THIRTY

Danny was standing beside his mate Evan, at the graveside of Evan's girlfriend Alicia, having just undergone the most harrowing two hours of his life. He knew Evan partly blamed Shelly for Alicia's murder. He didn't have the heart to tell him that it was Alicia who had been the one to introduce Shelly to the bastards. Or so Shelly had told him, though if he was honest with himself, he didn't trust anything Shelly said any more. He was missing her terribly, though, and knew if he saw her now, he would probably cave in. The last time he'd seen her, apart from dropping her stuff off at the hospital, while she'd been sleeping, she'd been a mess, lying on the floor covered in her own blood.

He remembered that first day in the hellhole, watching her stumbling towards the packing table, looking years older than she really was.

No, I won't. I'm not gonna start feeling sorry for her, he said sternly to himself. She's well gone, outta my life forever. And that's the way it's staying.

But God help her, she looked such a friggin' mess, the evil

bastards!

He yelped as Evan leaned on his bad side.

'Sorry,' Evan muttered.

'No, it's all right.' Danny gently rubbed his ribs through the borrowed black suit he wore. 'Are we going back in yet?'

The bar where Alicia's family had laid on food and drink, to see their daughter off, was just around the corner from the church-yard. They had gone there after the funeral, but then Evan had wanted to come back, and Danny wouldn't let him come on his own. For the last hour, they had been silently staring at Alicia's grave.

He wondered again at the phrase 'see her off'. Strange one that, but he guessed it had been around for years. Shrugging, he looked at Evan, who still hadn't answered him, but was staring at the beautiful array of flowers.

'Come on, mate, let's get going.'

This time Evan nodded, then surprised Danny when he spoke. 'She should have been here.'

'Who should have been here?' Danny blurted out, giving Evan a puzzled stare, a split second later realising who he meant just before Evan said loudly, 'Shelly, that's who.'

Danny sighed. 'I know, mate.'

'So where is she?'

'I don't know… Look, I'm sorry, honestly, I really haven't a clue where she is, and I don't think I want to. She's more bother than she's worth.'

'Danny, did you know what they were all up to in this…this cult thing they were into?'

'No, mate, I was as much in the dark as you were,' Danny said, defending himself from Evan's accusing tone.

Evan sighed. 'OK. I believe you. But hasn't it occurred to you how strange all of this is?'

'Cults are strange. Full of fucking weirdoes.' Sorry! He looked down at the grave, then up at the sky, as if waiting for a thunderbolt to strike him dead for blaspheming at a graveside.

'No, what I mean is, Danny, none of this has made the news, either the papers or the telly… For God's sake, it should be screaming out at us every time we switch the box on. Look at the way Alicia died - now that alone is worth newsprint. So why aren't they here now, shoving mikes into our faces, demanding to know what we know?'

Danny shrugged again. Looking around the empty graveyard as if expecting half a dozen reporters to jump out at them, he thought, he's right- why?

'Want to know what I think?' Evan went on before Danny could answer. 'I think there's some pretty high up bigwigs mixed up in all of this crap. I mean governments, world leaders, that kind of people, you know the sort I mean. That's why it's not in the papers or anywhere else, not even the internet. They can afford to keep it out. Same as it's always been, one rule for them, a different rule for us. I mean, the internet- how the hell can they keep it off there? Pretty spooky if you ask me.'

'True, mate.' He didn't mean to blurt out what he said next. As usual, he let it out before thinking it through. 'It's a fucking disgrace, that's what it is. I mean, the state of her body, and what the bastards did to her, it should have made world news, for Christ's sake!'

He forgot all about the bolt of lightning from above, and looked at Evan for confirmation. But Evan was staring at Alicia's grave again, seeing nothing but her ravaged body, her beautiful skin turned the colour of white marble and hanging in tatters. Tears dropped from his eyes and landed on the soil. He sobbed at the thought of what she had gone through. The pain must have been beyond belief.

'Oh, dear God, please look after her. She's good, my Alicia, please take care of her. No way did she deserve to die the way she did.' Gasping for air between sobs, his whole body shook.

'Right, that's it.' Danny pulled out his handkerchief and handed it to Evan. 'We are going to the pub now to toast Alicia's life, say goodbye to her folks and friends who came, and then we're going looking for Shelly, and I'll shake the fucking truth out of her. You mark my words, God damn it. Just you wait till I get my hands on her. She'll spill the beans then all right.'

Evan looked at him. Slowly he nodded, as a stubborn look stole over his face. 'Bet your fucking life we will.'

Reaching down, Evan snapped the head from one of the many floral tributes. Crushing the petals in his hand, he scattered them across the grave.

'Goodbye, Alicia. I love you. I promise to find the bastard. You'll see your day, I promise.'

Danny nodded. 'You bet, Alicia pet.' Together they turned and left the churchyard.

An hour later, after saying good bye to Alicia's family and promising that he would not under any circumstances be a stranger, Evan was walking to his flat with Danny.

'Why did they dye their hair black, Danny? I never understood that. Did they all have to look the same, every single one of them? And why weren't Alicia and Shelly in the monastery? Were they his…his…you know what I mean?'

Danny shrugged. 'I guess he did make them dye it black. Maybes the fucking creep has a thing for black hair. Who knows, with them sort of control freaks, could be any amount of reasons. Maybes his mother was blonde, and she beat him up. Maybes she had had black hair, and he fancied her. He was fucking crazy, man.'

'But why weren't they in the monastery like the others?' Evan repeated.

'I think that- just guessing here, mind, mate- they were sort of recruitment officers. Like encouraging young kids to become addicted, sort of dealers.'

'Drug dealers, you mean?' Evan's voice held the disgust he felt at the thought of Alicia and Shelly having anything at all to do with drugs, never mind dealing them. He and Danny had dabbled once a few years back, but the effect on Danny had been horrendous. Danny's attempts to take on every car on the A1 had been enough to scare them both off for life.

'Can't think of any other name for it.' Danny said with a shrug.

Evan thought this through for a minute, then said, 'You were in the monastery. How bad was it?'

'Bad, mate. Real fucking bad.'

'Tell me.'

But Danny's face had glazed over, remembering the state most of the kids were in. Dead souls looking out of eyes that were way too old for them. The eagerness with which they greeted the pill delivery every day. The scraps they were forced to eat. They way they all huddled together on a night for warmth. He shuddered.

'Tell me,' Evan prompted.

Danny shook his head. 'Another time, mate.' If Evan knew half of what had gone on in the monastery, it would probably be the tipping point that sent him right over the edge. 'We've got a lot of things to do. One thing though, if I ever catch that Leader twat, I'll rip his lips off, throw them in the fucking frying pan and make him eat the bastards.'

Evan stopped walking, picturing what Danny had just said.

He looked at his friend, and shook his head. Only Danny could come up with something like that. 'Gross!'

'He is that. Look, I'm gonna pop off home for a few minutes, grab some clothes and stuff, OK?'

'OK. Catch you in a bit.'

CHAPTER THIRTY-ONE

Brother David took the key from Aunt May's outstretched hand and opened the door. He frowned when he had to put his shoulder to it and push.

'What's the matter?' Aunt May asked, just as the door swung open. 'Oh my God,' she gasped. 'We've been bloody burgled.'

Brother David held his hand up to stop her rushing in. 'Careful. I'll go in first.'

'What have they done?'

'Just a minute.' He moved an old wooden coat hanger that had fallen across the doorway. It must have been the reason he hadn't been able to open the door. He stepped into chaos.

'What's wrong?' Smiler asked, coming up the path behind them with Aunt May's bags.

White-faced and shaking, Aunt May turned to him. 'We…we've been burgled, son.'

'No way!'

'Yes.' She nodded.

Stepping in front of her, Smiler followed Brother David into the house. For a moment he stood as transfixed as the monk, until a loud gasp from behind him broke the spell. Quickly, he turned and put his arm around Aunt May, who was sobbing into her hands.

'Who would do this?' she kept repeating.

'Morons,' Smiler stated.

Brother David moved into the kitchen, which was in pretty much the same state as the sitting room. Smashed furniture everywhere, the floor littered with broken crockery, hardly a bare place left to stand on.

In the sitting room, Smiler cleared a chair of torn pictures from three photograph albums. Being careful not to damage them further, he placed them on the table, leaving the chair clear for Aunt May to sit on. He looked around. Everything was broken, from the television to the ornaments on the sideboard. Nothing had been missed out. Plant pots had been smashed, their contents scattered everywhere soil was even clinging to the lampshade. And some of the flowered wall- paper was torn and hanging.

Smiler had a feeling that nothing had been stolen. Somehow this looked like a warning. He'd seen houses ransacked like this before, over drug money or if the person was a grass. He frowned, what the hell had Aunt May done to deserve this?

A moment later, he froze as Brother David came back in from the kitchen, stopped dead and, mouth hanging open, stared at the far wall. Slowly, a feeling of dread rising from his feet and spreading rapidly, Smiler turned.

On the wall, the outline of two horses back to back had been painted in gold paint.

Aunt May swung round. She stared at the outlines for a moment, her body stiffening.

'Aunt May,' Smiler said, his voice showing the worry that he was feeling.

As if Smiler's voice had brought her back to the here and now, she said, 'Why would somebody paint two unicorns on me bloody wall? If I get my hands on the sods, I'll strangle the life outta them.' Aunt May was shaking with anger as she looked around her ruined home, then back up at the paintings on the wall.

'They are unicorns,' Smiler muttered, seeing the horns he had missed at first. 'I thought they were horses.' Turning back to Brother David, he said, 'What does it mean?'

Brother David swallowed, looked at Smiler and said, 'In the Leader's apartment at the monastery, he had two gold back to back unicorns on the ceilings.'

Smiler shivered. 'He's warning us, isn't he?'

'Looks like it. Never did understand the reason for them.' Brother David's mind was in a turmoil. How to keep Aunt May safe? How to keep Smiler safe? Was the message actually from the Leader, or from the ones who had hurt Aunt May? They were obviously connected in some way to the Leader, but they seemed to have their own agenda.

Smiler pulled his phone out and dialled Kristina Clancy's number. Hearing what had happened, she promised to be there as soon as possible, and told him not to touch anything. As he put his phone away, he looked guiltily at the photograph albums.

'Er, sit down, Aunt May. And we, we…er, she said don't touch anything, OK?'

Brother David walked to the door that led to the stairs. 'I'll just have a quick look up here.'

He was back in moments. 'It's fine.'

'You sure?' Aunt May asked.

'Promise, Aunt May. Everything's all right up there.'

'They might have seen us coming before they got to upstairs… I'll just go and see how Tiny is.' Smiler was out of the door before either of them could say anything.

CHAPTER THIRTY-TWO

Standing outside the police station in London, Mike stared at the building. He'd been here for a good fifteen minutes, and knew something was not quite right. Something was missing from the picture, and he couldn't quite put his finger on it. He looked around again, just as a pigeon swooped overhead and flew in the direction of the bird lady.

Only she wasn't there.

That's it, he thought, snapping his fingers, she's what's missing. No flash of red against the grey building.

He frowned. But she's always here.

Hope she's all right.

The bird lady, who everyone in the station had nicknamed Little Red Riding Hood, had been part of the landscape for as long as anyone could remember - but she left his mind as quickly as she'd entered it when he saw Tony come out of the station and turn left. Mike was pleased to see that he was alone. That was what he'd wanted -no one to know they had met up, no phone calls that could be traced. He hadn't expected to strike it lucky this soon, and had been quite prepared to hover for days to find him.

Mike crossed the road and caught up with him. He was less than five feet behind Tony when he changed his plan. Instead of confronting him right off, and demanding to know which puzzle piece he was in this hopeless jigsaw, Mike decided to follow him for a while and see what happened.

Five minutes later, Tony turned down a side street. Mike fell in behind a party of early revellers going their way, obviously a hen party of a dozen or so young women dressed as bunny girls. As the street narrowed, Mike found himself in the middle of the girls.

'Hey, you gorgeous man, wanna come with us?' a tiny red-head asked, exaggeratedly batting her eyelids at him as the other girls laughed. She had huge breasts. Surely they cant possibly be real? Mike was thinking, as he tried to tare his eyes away.

A tall blonde caught his eye. 'Come on a good time guaranteed.' she giggled.

'No thanks.' Mike smiled at them, hoping the noise they were making wouldn't attract Tony's attention, as he disentangled his arm from the redhead's.

'Have it your way, gorgeous, but I promise you don't know what you're missing.' The tall blonde winked at him and blew a kiss as she led the way through a club doorway with twinkling lights and a huge flashing neon sign.

He gave her a quick smile, then they were gone from his mind as he saw Tony turn into a shop doorway. Hurrying up, he saw that it was an old second-hand bookshop. He hovered in front of the window for a moment, but it was impossible to see past the piles of second-hand books that filled the window.

Should I go in or wait until he comes back out?

He glanced quickly around. No one suspicious-looking lurking in the street.

OK, do what you came to do!

He pushed the door open. Inside was quite dark and gloomy. It took a moment or two for his eyes to adjust. Then he spotted the door at the far end, and another window piled high with books. The shop had two frontages and an entrance in two streets.

Bastard!

He knew I was following him.

How the hell? But he knew that Tony was nothing if not resourceful. Probably clocked me as soon as I reached the station. Bet he even knew what time I got on the train back home.

And here's me thinking I'm practically invisible… Damn!

Quickly, Mike ran through the store. An old man and a teenager, both wearing the same frown, watched him pass.

His hand ready to slap the handle, the breath was suddenly knocked out of him as he was hit with a rugby tackle from behind. Mike landed on the floor. Quickly he flipped onto his back and launched his left fist, connecting with the chin of the man who had brought him down.

On his back, Mike saw there was another one. Against two, he was at a severe disadvantage, but he'd taken more than one on before. He used every fighting technique that he knew. Throwing his head back, then quickly forward, he nutted the one he had just chinned, rendering him semi-conscious. Jumping up, he turned to the other man, who held a large sword and was about to bring it down on Mike's head. Stepping quickly under his raised arm, Mike delivered a knife-hand strike, crushing his cartilage in seconds. The sword slid out of the man's hands and fell with a loud clatter onto the tiled floor.

For a moment, Mike was stunned as the man who, eyes bulging and staring at him, reached slowly for his own throat and made a strange gurgling noise as he collapsed in a heap on the floor. Stepping back Mike stood on the unconscious man's hand and heard bones crunch in at least two of his fingers.

Inwardly Mike cringed, but felt no qualms this time. The broken fingers would send a message. The gauntlet was down. It had after all been a case of him or them.

The sound of sirens coming his way urged him on. In seconds, he was out of the bookshop and walking briskly in the opposite direction.

At the top of the street, he turned and watched as half a dozen officers jumped out of two police cars and ran into the shop.

So that's it then, he thought.

Knowing that their next move would be to publicly discredit

him and officially declare him on the run, he headed for Tony's flat.

No pussyfooting around now. The owner of the shop and the kid had seen him.

There was nothing left to lose.

CHAPTER THIRTY-THREE

As Smiler walked down Jill's path, he heard Tiny bark from the back garden. 'Hi, mutt, it's me,' Smiler said loudly. Tiny was silent for a moment, then recognising Smiler's voice he went into a frenzied fit of excited barking.

The front door opened before he reached it, and Jill smiled at him. 'Thought it might be you, Smiler, the way he's carrying on. Come on in.'

Following her into the house, Smiler was wondering how to tell her what had happened. He knew Jill could be a bit awkward sometimes. He shrugged, and said to her back as they reached the sitting room door, 'Aunt May's been robbed.'

'What?' Jill spun round.

'Well, we don't really know if she's been robbed yet, but somebody's been in and trashed the place.'

'Is Aunt May all right? Does she know?'

'Oh, she just got out of hospital 'bout an hour ago. We walked right into the whole mess.'

'What! You mean May actually walked into her house and

saw it all wrecked?'

'Well, yes.' Smiler felt himself becoming agitated. She wasn't giving him a chance to tell her what happened.

'Where is she now?' Jill demanded.

'At home.' Just listen, will you? he thought.

'Jesus!' Turning, Jill ran out of the house. Just as she left, Smiler heard her mutter to herself, 'That wasn't supposed to happen.'

Puzzled by what she'd said, or by what he thought she'd said, and slightly annoyed, Smiler unhooked Tiny's lead from a peg on the back door. Going in to the garden, he was pounced on by Tiny who showered him with dog kisses.

'Come on, boy.' Smiler patted Tiny, then surprised himself by giving the dog a cuddle. Stepping back, he looked at the dog and sighed. 'Let's go. Aunt May needs cheering up.'

They reached home just as Kristina arrived. 'How bad is it, Smiler?' she asked, jumping out of the car.

'Bad.' Smiler nodded solemnly.

'Damn.'

Two male police officers got out of the car and followed Smiler and Kristina down the path. They reached the door just as Aunt May and Jill, who had ran down the back way, came out of the house.

'Hello, love,' Aunt May said to Kristina. 'You got here quick.'

'The causeway was clear, thank God. How are you?'

But Aunt May's attention was taken up by Tiny who, refusing to be ignored, was standing on his hind legs, one paw resting on Aunt May's shoulder and the other one batting the air. 'OK, OK, good dog, pleased to see you an' all, you bloody ugly hound.'

Everyone laughed as Aunt May ruffled Tiny's head.

'Good job he doesn't know what you're saying,' Jill put in, but Aunt May had turned to Kristina.

'Me, I'm fine. The bloody house isn't, though! Take a look in there. Bloody hooligans. Think they can do what they want these days. A good slap around the chops, that's what they bloody well need. But oh no, the bloody do-gooders won't have that, will they? Course they won't. It's not their bloody houses that's getting trashed, is it?'

'Come on, May,' Jill said, nodding at Kristina. 'I'm taking her up mine for a bit, until your lot are finished, then we'll get on with sorting the place out.'

'Fine.' Kristina smiled. 'Catch you later, Aunt May,' she said - with the emphasis on 'Aunt'.

Aunt May smiled. She knew Kristina saw Jill as a rival, and she had been rather disappointed when she and Mike had split up- but now she was back.

I only hope Mike makes the right choice, she thought, heading up the path after Jill.

Inside, Kristina surveyed the mess. 'Well, they've certainly gone to town, haven't they?'

'Uh huh,' Brother David replied, as the two officers started dusting for fingerprints.

'Any idea why this would happen?'

'It's got to be the same people who hit her, hasn't it? Too much of a coincidence for it not to be.'

'Yes, that's what I think… But what do they think she has, or knows about them?'

Brother David shook his head. 'Haven't got a clue. She's hardly steps foot off the island, apart from the odd trip to Berwick and a few holidays with friends a couple of times a year down Norfolk way.'

'Don't blame her, wish I could live here.' Kristina didn't add, 'with Mike', though they both knew that was what she was thinking.

Feeling useless hanging around with nothing to do until the police were finished- though he guessed, rightly, there wouldn't be a lot they could do, only fools leave fingerprints these days- Smiler took Tiny for a walk. Most of the day-trippers had gone home, and the island was pretty quiet. This was just how he liked it.

As he headed up towards the castle, the only other person on the road was a youngish woman in denim jacket and jeans, with a haversack slung over her shoulder. She was about fifty yards in front of him and walking fast.

Smiler was wondering what Jill had meant when she'd said, 'That wasn't supposed to happen.'

'She definitely said it,' he muttered. 'I know she did. But why? She must have meant something else.' Puzzling over it, he carried on up the road.

He blinked a moment later when he saw something that looked like a purse drop from the woman's haversack as she shifted it along her shoulder.

Suddenly he was back in the midst of London, forcing his way through the crowds, praying that no one picked up the dropped purse before he did, hoping that there was plenty of money in it for him to party. He was desperately in need of a fix. The purse was manna from heaven.

Reaching the spot where he had seen the purse fall, he knelt down, a solid rock in a raging river. He pushed his arms against the tide of legs around him, begging, pleading, praying for the purse to be still there when he reached the right spot. Blindly, he scrabbled around with his fingers. At first there was nothing - then his fingers closed around the purse.

Suddenly, Tiny started barking. Smiler blinked and straightened up. He looked in puzzlement at the purse in his hand, wondering where it had come from, then at the back of the retreating woman. For a moment, he hesitated.

Got to give it back, a small voice said in his head.

No, it's mine. I found it.

Got to give it back, the voice repeated.

He shook himself. 'Course I have to,' he muttered, remembering her dropping it. 'Might be all she's got.' Smiler well knew what it was like to wake up penniless.

'Hey! Hey, lady! You dropped your purse,' he shouted, jumping up and running after her.

She turned when he shouted again. Recognising what he held in his hand, she waited until he reached her. Breathing a sigh of relief, she held her hand out. 'Thank you very much.'

'No problem. You need to make sure the zip is fastened on your backpack,' he said, handing the purse over.

'Please wait.' She pulled a ten pound note out of the purse and held it out. 'For you.'

'No, thank you.'

'Please take it. There's more than a hundred quid in here, I would have lost the whole lot if you hadn't found it. Not everyone's as honest as you.'

Smiler backed away. 'No, really, it's all right.' He moved out of her reach and, turning, quickly walked away.

'I'll give it to charity, then.'

'OK.' Nodding, he speeded up. He had gone only a few yards when the voice in his head said, 'Well done, Smiler.' He knew the voice belonged to Rita.

Feeling a very rare warm tingle inside, he headed for home. The idea that he had just donated to some charity completely fascinated him. He couldn't remember ever feeling this good.

He had reached the gate when he had a flashback- Tiny

searching for Aunt May.

Tiny finding Aunt May!

'Yes!'

He ran down the path and into the house.

'Whoa,' Kristina yelled, 'we can't have him in here. He'll destroy any evidence that there is.'

'No, you don't understand, Tiny will find them. He's brilliant at tracking. He found Aunt May, didn't he?' He looked eagerly at Aunt May for confirmation.

Aunt May raised her eyebrows. 'Did he?' She patted the dog's head. 'So it was you. Clever dog.'

'Yes, and he'll be able to lead us to the swines who did this. I bettcha, honest he will. You should have seen him tearing around the village looking for Aunt May. You've gotta give him a try. She might have died if Tiny hadn't found her.'

Kristina mulled it over for a moment then, shrugging, said, 'OK, why not. We can't even find a print here. So give it a go, let him off the lead so he can sniff around.'

Excited that he had been the one to come up with a plan, Smiler slipped Tiny's lead off. 'Go, boy.'

At first Tiny was more interested in trying to smother Aunt May in kisses, then Smiler shoved a couple of torn photographs under his nose. Tiny moved his head then, sniffing, swung back to the photographs.

'Find, Tiny, find,' Smiler repeated over and over, until suddenly Tiny started running round the sitting room, stopping to sniff at various places, before running for the door and starting to howl. Quickly, Smiler slipped his lead on, and opened the door.

'I'll come too,' Kristina said.

Together they retraced the steps that Smiler and Tiny had just made on their way back a few minutes ago.

'Hope he's not following me.'

Kristina looked oddly at him. 'You trying to crack a joke?'

Smiler blushed and hid a hint of a smile.' It's just that this is the way we came back just now.'

'OK, we'll see if he goes further than you did. Who knows? He may lead us right to the culprit.'

'He will, dogs are much cleverer than people give them credit for.'

'We'll see.'

A few minutes later, without losing steam, Tiny took them right up to the castle.

On the way up the long windy road that led to the castle, Kristina made the mistake of commenting on the fantastic view, and how grand the castle looked against the sky.

Smiler paused a moment, and pointed at another, much bigger castle, across the water on the mainland. 'That's Bamburgh Castle.'

'I know.' Kristina smiled.

'This castle was built in 1550, around about the same time as the priory fell out of use. Stones from the priory were dragged up and used to build some of it. In the eighteenth century, the castle was briefly occupied by Jacobite rebels, but was quickly recaptured by soldiers who imprisoned the rebels. They dug themselves out, and hid for nine days close to Bamburgh Castle, before making good their escape… Did you know that this castle has been used in films?' Ignoring Kristina's sigh, he went on, 'Yes, Roman Polanski used it for The Tragedy of Macbeth in 1971. Good film. They----'

'Well, I never knew that at all,' Kristina put in quickly, before he could go on.

'There's more.'

Kristina held up her hand. 'I'm sure there is, love, but it'll have to keep. We're here now, and we need to find out who's hiding in here. That's supposing the dog's right.'

Reaching the door, Kristina took out her badge. 'Before we go in, are we sure they don't let rooms out?'

'Just to certain guests, I think that's what Aunt May said. Her friend's a cleaner here.'

A few minutes later, they were inside the castle and finding it hard to keep up with Tiny as he dragged them along corridor after corridor. He finally came to rest outside a door that he started to scratch.

'Oh,' Kristina said, stop him before he digs through the door, 'they'll sue for damages.'

'Stop it. Down, boy.' Smiler pushed Tiny's paw down.

Obediently, Tiny lay down. Pressing his nose to the bottom of the door, he began to sniff. Jumping up a moment later, he howled.

'Guess this is it, then. Hope he hasn't been chasing a friggin' cat.' She looked at Smiler.

'No… Well- I don't think so. No. Definitely not a cat.'

'Hmm.' Looking unconvinced, Kristina knocked on the door. A moment later it opened, revealing the occupant.

'You! Smiler said in disbelief.

CHAPTER THIRTY-FOUR

Shelly was perched on a bar stool, her short black skirt showing a lot of bare thigh as she crossed her legs. Picking up her glass, she took a sip of what looked like gin. Between her and the girl serving behind the bar, who thought she was looking for her boyfriend to give him a surprise and catch him with another girl, it was water. For what was to come, she needed a very clear head

There was no getting away from the fact that the place was a dive- sticky carpets, sticky bar, noisy clientele. Loud music was leaking out of the door into the dark. But it was just the sort of place that she wanted. The sort of place where recruits were picked up and introduced to the little yellow pills.

Guess summer's on the wane, she thought, looking at the clock on the bar wall. Eight o' clock, and the sky was growing dark already, though that was probably the storm clouds that were brewing. Still no flaming sign of what she was looking for, though. Perhaps it was time to move on to the next dump. She slid off the stool and, raising her glass to the barmaid, she drank the water and headed for the door.

She spent the next hour touring half a dozen bars, a couple full to the brim on a buy one, get one free night, the others just about empty. With no sightings of anyone who looked like they might be involved with the Leader, she decided to go back to the hotel.

She took a slow walk along the High Street. A few people were about, but it was mostly pretty quiet. She was passing a hotel that looked a whole lot better than hers, when at last she had her first bit of luck. The trio she was looking for stepped out of a car right in front of her. For a brief moment she was stunned but managing to hold it together, she took a step forward.

He'd cut his hair, but she would recognise him anywhere. He oozed arrogance. It flowed from him in waves. You are the shit beneath my shoes, his body language screamed.

Inside she was burning. Her need for revenge became even stronger than she ever thought it could as, outwardly calm, she passed within three yards of them. At the side of the hotel was an alleyway. She ducked inside and leaned against the wall and took a deep breath.

How the hell did I do that? Walk right on past them?

Her heart was pounding in her ears, but she was smiling.

If I can walk past them like that, then I can do what I plan to do! I can do anything I fucking well want to.

The next moment she changed her mind. Can't do it… No way.

The trembling in her hands transferred to her whole body. If I can score, at least I'll stop shaking. Then I'll be able to do it.

Bastards. It's their fault I'm addicted.

Should have picked some up. Certain that creep in the red hoodie at the first pub was working it. Pity he only had dope on him.

'Can't do it,' she mumbled.

'Yes, you can.' She looked quickly around. There was nobody there. Then the voice came again, from somewhere inside of her. 'You can do this.'

Freaked out for a moment, she froze. It was a voice she didn't recognise, certainly not her own. What the hell is in those little yellow fuckers that the bastards are filling the streets with?

'You can do it.' The voice faded away on the last word.

Who?

But there wasn't even an echo. Must have imagined it, going fucking crazy now.

OK, if I'm losing the plot, I might as well go for it. Got nothing else to lose now. Everything else is gone.

'Danny,' she muttered. Even the sound of his name tore her apart. Taking a deep breath, she squared her shoulders and, trying to stem the trembling in her hands, looked round the corner.

Of the Leader and the Chinese guard there was no sign, but the other one, the English sadist, was talking to the concierge.

This is it. A chance I might not get again.

Her plan had been a poor one, but all she'd been able to come up with- to get inside whatever place they were using now, and hopefully take whatever chance she could to murder the bastards, before they recognised her.

Taking her insulin pen out of her bag, she took the top off and wound it to the full dose, which would be lethal to a non-diabetic. Armed and ready, she stepped round the corner, keeping her head down, because it was the eyes that would give her away. If her eyes once met with the fiend's, he would know her immediately.

As she reached him, she wobbled, tripped over and fell against him. Quickly, she jabbed him in the back of his ankle and pressed the plunger. Before he turned, the pen was back in her pocket.

CHAPTER THIRTY-FIVE

Mike sat in the café opposite Tony's flat, facing the window. He wore a flat cap pulled well down on his brow. He expected his face would be flashed all over the ten o' clock news, but that was a good few hours away yet. As well as dragging the truth out of Tony, he needed somewhere to hide out for a while.

The café was one he'd visited two or three times before when waiting for Tony to make an appearance. He was late as usual, but the proprietor didn't seemed to recognise him. If he had, the cops would have been here long ago. It was probably the only good thing that had happened in a while.

Pictures of 40s and 50s film stars were scattered around the walls, some of them long dead now, the rest probably hidden away in some old folks' home. Comfortable brown leather armchairs and long low coffee tables with magazines scattered on them filled the room.

All very nice, Mike thought, but the coffee's shite!

In the corner a young girl, obviously a student, was updating her Facebook page, humming along annoyingly with the jarring music coming out of her headphones. An old couple somewhere in their eighties, who still looked very much in love, were sat in the opposite corner.

Love? What is love? Mike thought. The love from a mother and a father? Well, that I've never known. Unwanted from day one.

Sometimes Mike wondered about his mother - who she was, where she was. And his father, what was he doing now?

What had he ever done?

Were they just a pair of kids when I was born?

Do they ever wonder about me?

Do I really want to know?

But the older he got, the less he thought of them, though he guessed that the wanting to know would never go away. The only thing he did know was that he had been in the home practically from birth, and that two foster homes hadn't worked out. 'Guess I was lucky the third time around,' he muttered.

He'd promised himself that one day he would go looking, but it had never seemed like the right time. One thing, poor Dave won't ever go looking. Wonder if the poor sod still has the nightmares. He remembered the time when they were about ten years old, when Dave, who had always seemed so very quiet and withdrawn, had told him and Tony of the terrible things that had happened to him for as long as he could remember.

Guess he and Smiler have a lot in common. Mike sighed and chewed on his inner lip.

But that day had not only changed Dave, whose spirit seemed a whole lot lighter when he at last opened up to Mike and Tony and got everything off his chest. He had finally started to smile. It had also changed Mike, bringing a darker element to his soul when he found out how his friend had suffered.

Tony, though, Mike thought, he had known love and lost it, one dark, rainy night when his parents' car had crashed into a lorry on the M1. Tony had sobbed as he'd told his tale to them, one summer night when they were camping in Aunt May's garden.

Mike sighed. No way could Tony be involved with the bastards. Don't care how much evidence points his way, there has to be an explanation. And one way or another I'm going to get it.

Rising, he moved to the counter and paid the bill, then went outside, nodding at the old couple as he passed them. Standing on the corner outside the café, he lit a cigarette and stared up at Tony's window.

Where are you? he thought. And just how deep into this bloody shit are you?

He threw the finished cigarette away. As he did so, the light in Tony's apartment went on. 'How the hell did he get past me?' Mike wondered, as he quickly crossed the road and entered the building.

CHAPTER THIRTY-SIX

Shelly tried to scramble up as the guard turned to help her. He took her arm, and began pulling her up.

Inside she was shaking, terrified in case the insulin hadn't worked. But suddenly he let go of her and started to sway. His knees gave way first -then slowly, silently, he started to crumple. When he came face to face with Shelly, he was totally disorientated, but for a brief moment he looked into her eyes and knew her.

Quickly, she made it to her feet and walked away, just as the driver came running round the car to see what had happened.

Dear me, she thought with a smile. That poor man must have had a heart attack.

Happens all the time!

CHAPTER THIRTY-SEVEN

Evan sat on his favourite chair, staring at the blank TV screen, wondering where the hell Danny was, staring for long minutes at the photograph he held in his hand of the smiling Alicia. He kissed the photograph, before pressing it against his heart. A single tear ran down his face, and that was all it took. Suddenly he was sobbing his heart out.

'Where are you, Danny?' he shouted, throwing a cup from the coffee table in front of him at the wall, where it shattered on impact spewing dark brown liquid over the wall. It seemed everywhere he looked in the flat, all he could see was Alicia.

'Can't stand it... For fuck's sake, Danny, hurry up. Got to get out of here.'

Danny was on his way to Evan's flat, running about ten minutes late, having been back to his own flat to change out of the too-tight black suit into jeans and navy blue shirt. He had packed an extra pair of jeans, underwear and a couple of t-shirts in his holdall, just as Evan had said to do.

He was all for going after Shelly as Evan wanted, but couldn't help but think that it was far too soon.

And so un-Evanlike, he thought, passing the bench where, only a week ago, the milkman had woken him into a totally different world from the one he'd fallen asleep in.

Evan is the calm one, the wait and see what happens one, and now he's got crackerjack me traipsing off on a wild goose chase!

He's not thinking straight. The poor sod hasn't even had time to grieve yet.

Passing the local fish and chip shop, the smell lured him through the door. Some nice cod and chips for supper before we set off to wherever the hell we're going to. Bloody lovely.

The owner, a tall, bald headed man, was stirring the chips around in the fryer when he looked up and saw Danny in the small queue of four or five people. He dropped the scoop, and for a moment his jaw also dropped. Watching this, Danny felt prickles run over his scalp. What's up with him, like?

Oh God! He's gonna kick off big time. I just know it. The smell of trouble had replaced that of the fish and chips. Danny put his head down. All he wanted was his supper.

Suddenly the manager leaned over the counter and said loudly, 'What the hell are you doing out on the streets, useless bastard? After what you did to that poor lass Alicia, they should have thrown away the fucking key.'

Aghast, Danny muttered, 'It wasn't me.' Swallowing hard, he

said again, more loudly, 'Honest, it wasn't me.'

'So it wasn't you running along the street the other day yelling your fucking head off, saying she's dead?'

'Well…well, yes, but----'

Suddenly everyone in the shop tried to get away from Danny as if he was carrying some horrendous plague, and piled into the corner.

'Honest, it wasn't me.' He implored the people to believe him. 'I just found her in my bed. Why can't you believe me? I had enough trouble with the friggin' coppers.'

One of the customers, a young girl with a ginger pony-tail, muttered, 'Creep.' The other customers, four of them young men, mouthed their agreement.

'Go on, piss off outta here,' the manager said, with a sideways toss of his head in the direction of the door. 'Don't know how you're even out on the streets. Bloody disgrace.'

'So it is,' an old woman said, poking her head out from behind one of the young men.

Danny began to back away. 'I only wanted some fish and chips,' he muttered, frowning at them all.

'Well, you're not getting any here, so piss off. And I'm calling the cops now.'

'Disgraceful.' The old woman popped her head out again. 'It's not safe on the streets any more, with the likes of lunatics like you running around.'

Distraught Danny yelled, 'I've told you it wasn't me. I just found her didn't I.'

'Well, that's not what I heard. An animal wouldn't do what you did to that poor girl. Get out.'

Shaking his head, Danny walked out of the door. As he took one step outside, he swung back and yelled, 'Shove yer fish and chips up yer fucking arse.'

He could hear them mouthing off as he crossed the road. Cheeky bastards, he thought, looking from side to side to see if anyone had heard the commotion. I'm gonna get the blame for this for ever, no one's ever gonna believe I had nothing to do with it. Shit!

No way, man.

How many times do I have to say it wasn't me?

The coppers are gonna have to make a statement, put it in the paper or something. Tell them I was a fucking victim an' all. It's just not fair. It wasn't me. It was them!

He reached the other side of the road and was halfway over the grassy bank in front of Evan's flat when he heard a loud explosion. Gasping in shock, he looked up at the second floor flat as the windows instantaneously shattered, followed seconds later by huge tongues of fire.

For a very brief moment, he froze staring up at the fire. His heart started to pound as he realised who's flat was on fire, all thought of his aching ribs disappeared as he ran screaming, towards the flats.

He was stopped near the entrance by two men who had been passing by at the very moment of the blast, and had just managed to pick themselves up from the ground.

'You can't go in there, son,' one of them said, grabbing hold of his arm, while the other caught him by his collar. He could feel the

man who had hold of his arm shaking as if he was having a fit. Then people started running out of the building, screaming and yelling for other family members.

'But my mate, he's in there waiting for me. I've got to see if he's all right.'

'He'll be out in a minute, look, everyone's out now… Well, just about, I think.'

Starting to tremble himself with shock, Danny looked at him and slowly shook his head. 'Not Evan, he'll not be coming out now. Not ever. Oh God.' He hung his head in despair.

'Why do you think that, son?' asked the man who had grabbed his collar, and who was now holding his other arm.

"Cause…'cause it's his flat that blew. He's never coming outta there. Not alive.' A moment later, Danny passed out and collapsed onto the ground.

CHAPTER THIRTY-EIGHT

Two hours later, a traumatised Danny was discharged from the hospital in handcuffs. He was taken to the police station, to the same room he'd been in not so long ago.

He was sitting in the chair, biting his lip, wondering if it was going to be the same two coppers from hell, when the door opened, He groaned to see the same woman. 'Oh, no,' he muttered.

Kristina smiled as she walked to the table and sat down facing him. Out of her handbag she took a notepad and a pen, then looked up and smiled again.

Well, that's a big improvement on the last time, Danny thought. It was hard to tell which one was the friggin' worst. Or is she just showing her teeth?

That could be bad! He sighed. The story of his life, up shit creek without a paddle. Again.

She said nothing, just folded her hands on the desk and looked at him. Danny squirmed in his chair. The door opened again, and a man Danny had never seen before came in and sat next to Kristina.

'This is an informal interview, Danny, hence no recorder, nor solicitor, although there is one available if you feel the need. What we mostly want to know is how you keep turning up whenever there is a murder?' Kristina said, her eyebrows raised.

'Bad luck?' Danny quipped with half a smile. Then, as usual, he wanted to bite his tongue.

'This is not a joke, young man,' said Detective Sergeant Cox.

'I know it's not,' Danny snapped. 'My best mate's lying in the fucking hospital with hardly any skin on, for Christ's sake. Nobody knows if he'll even live till tomorrow, and you lot have got me in here! I should be there with Evan.'

'So, why the levity?' Katrina asked.

'I don't fucking know.'

'Think it's funny, all these people dying around you?' Cox asked.

'No… What do you mean, 'all these people'… Evan?' Danny's heart flipped. Had the bastards kept him here all this time, knowing Evan was dead?

'No, he's still hanging in. Though God knows how- the young couple in the flat next door didn't make it,' Katrina said.

'Look, please believe me. I know next to nowt about any of this. It's like I'm caught up in a fucking nightmare. You already know that I was a prisoner in that hellhole, you know I nearly got my ribs caved in… Does it look like I'm part of whatever the hell's going on?' Danny hung his head in despair and stared at the floor.

Kristina and Cox looked at each other. Kristina shook her head, sighed, and said, 'Is there anything you can tell us about your time in the monastery, anything you missed out before? The smallest detail that might not seem important to you?'

'No, nothing. I've already told you what happened in that dump. OK? I'm having nightmares about the damn place. Jesus Christ, are you friggin' well trying to add to them? And how long do I have to keep these on if I'm not under arrest?'

They both nodded, as Cox, standing up and pushing his chair in, said, 'Understandable, but sometimes people forget things. I'll go and get the keys.'

'Forget that horror! Never,' Danny muttered, more to himself than Kristina.

'All right, I understand,' Kristina said. 'But please understand this. Anything, anything at all that could help us bring the ones responsible for this to justice, anything at all that you can think of, some small detail, something you heard while you were in there that might not seem to be important, would be a help.'

Change the frigging record, will you? Danny was thinking. We've already been here.

Cox came back in with the keys. Gesturing for Danny to stand up, he unlocked the cuffs, then sat back down.

Sighing, Danny also sat down, thinking, It looks like Twit and Twat still aren't finished with me.

'Right,' he said, before either of them could speak. 'If anything comes up, I'll tell you. In return I need you to tell people that I had nothing to do with Alicia's murder, please. They all think I did it. Now they'll think I blew the friggin' flats up as well. It's just not fair, you've gotta catch them bastards… Nearly got stoned outta the fish shop tonight, for Christ's sake. The bloody fish shop! Where next, eh? You gotta tell people… Can I go now?'

Kristina shrugged. 'Can't see why not.'

'You believe me?' Danny stared at Kristina in amazement.

'Guess so.' Cox answered for her. 'Better move, quick before we change our minds and find a reason to keep you here. And judging from what's gone on around you in the last few days, trust me, it won't be too hard.'

Danny was up out of his seat in moments and heading for the door. He turned and said, 'Any chance of a lift to the hospital, seeing as I was already there and you brought me here? I really need to be with Evan.'

Cox stood up. 'Why not. I'm going there, anyhow. If you'd like to wait out front, I won't be long.'

Danny nodded as he closed the door behind him. Leaning on it, he puffed out his cheeks. Not believing his luck that they seemed to believe him, he headed for outside.

Inside the office, Kristina tapped her pen on the pad, looked up at Cox, and asked, 'So what do you really think?'

'Honestly?' He shrugged. 'I think he's probably one of the most unluckiest people in the world.'

'I agree. Actually, I feel quite sorry for him. There's also not a lot we can do, press-wise, seeing as there's now a tight lid on the whole operation. Strange, don't you think?'

'Very. Personally, I wish Mike had told us a hell of lot more than he did.'

'Any word from him yet?'

'No. Not a peep.'

She shook her head. 'Me neither. I also think it's even more strange that within less than half an hour, that fill-in shop keeper we arrested up at the castle was walking free, virtually before we even had time to question the prat. Don't you?'

'I thought when you brought him in he seemed very cocksure about it all.'

Kristina nodded. 'Yeah, he practically laughed in my face when I arrested him.'

Cox tutted. 'I've searched the internet. Just the same old conspiracy theories. Problem is, a lot of them sound plausible.'

'Anything at all on the little bit Mike did give away?'

'A few things. We'll talk later, OK? I'll get this hapless sod back to the hospital.'

Danny was waiting beside Cox's car, wondering what the hell could happen next. In a short time, he'd just about lost everything and everyone he loved in the world. Please God don't let Evan die. Whatever I've done for all this to happen, I'm sorry. Please, please. Don't let him die. He crossed his fingers like a child and squeezed.

Cox came out of the station, pressing the button on his car fob. 'Get in, Danny.'

A blonde police woman on her way into the station gave Danny a filthy look. He quickly got into the car. 'See what I mean? Even your copper mates think I'm guilty. Bet you anything you like they'll be following me about and I'll get the fucking blame if somebody nicks a pint of milk off the step.'

'OK, I'll put the word around the station that you're an innocent victim in all this mess. All right?'

'Thanks,' Danny muttered.

They reached the hospital, and Danny jumped out of the car. 'Thanks, again,' he said, before shutting the door and hurrying into the hospital.

Watching him go, Cox realised he hadn't been joking when he'd told Kristina that Danny was the unluckiest person on the planet. He also guessed that Danny hadn't realised the bomb was probably meant for him more than for his friend.

CHAPTER THIRTY-NINE

At the very moment that Evan's window blew out, Mike was turning the handle of Tony's door. Surprised to find it unlocked, he flung the door wide and stepped in, to see Tony sitting on a chair facing the door with two glasses of ale in his hands.

Tony's flat was a typical successful male's pad. Huge music system, an even bigger TV, bar in the corner, laptop open and ready on the table, and everything matching in shades of red and brown.

'Took your time, mate,' Tony said. 'How long did you plan on drinking that vile stuff he calls coffee?'

Mike blinked in surprise. 'You knew I was there?'

'Of course.' Tony turned his head towards the window that ran the full width of the room, from which you could clearly see right into the coffee shop. The kid was still sitting with her laptop, fingers going at high speed, and the old couple were now holding hands.

'So. You taking the piss, or what?' Mike strode in and sat on the chair facing Tony.

'No, just waiting to see if the coast was clear. I've been given the week off, or twenty-four hours - depends how long it takes to catch you. Obviously, I'm not allowed anywhere near the case. I think I convinced them that you wouldn't be stupid enough to show up here… But here you are.' He held one of the beers out to Mike who, grim-faced, took it and put it down on the table.

'Why did you do it, Mike? For Christ's sake, you didn't have to kill him, you could have knocked the bastard out. But no, as usual you went way over the top.'

'Over the top?' Mike yelled. 'The bastards were out to kill me. What the hell did you expect me to do?'

Tony shook his head, sighed and went on, 'Actually, in another five minutes or so I was coming over. It's only a matter of time before they get sick and come here looking for you, to slap you with a murder charge.'

'Think I don't know that?'

'So why are you still hanging around?'

Mike jumped up. Grabbing Tony by the throat, he hauled him out of his chair. Ignoring the pint of beer that spilt over the pair of them, he shook Tony. 'Stop it, right now. I want answers.'

'To what?'

'You know what.'

'Just put me down, OK? We all know you're bigger and tougher than me. That was proved a long time ago.'

Mike narrowed his eyes. 'You bearing a grudge, or what? Is

that what all this is about?'

'No! No, of course not. Just let me go.'

Mike let go and pushed Tony back onto his chair.

Tony straightened his shirt, and tried to brush the moisture out of his trousers.

'I'm waiting,' Mike snarled.

'OK. It's not what you think, nothing personal… I love you, for Christ's sake, you're my brother. And actually, I take offence that you would even suggest something like that.'

'Just fucking get on with it, before I lose it completely, eh, Tony? Enough pissing around. I know you're involved with that bunch who've been in control for centuries. The same bunch that think they are our lords and masters, the same bunch that are into everything that is filthy and fucking vile about the human race.'

'You always were the one for conspiracy theories, Mike, but where the hell have you dragged that one up from?' Tony laughed. 'But forget it, OK? You're already in enough trouble as it is. Now we have to figure how to get you safely out of London. Even out of England.'

Mike looked suspiciously at Tony. 'Out of England? No way!'

'But----'

'No buts about it Tony. I've got things to do. No! Enough of trying to wriggle out of it, I want answers. Ah, yes - before we go into that, any reason why you weren't answering my phone when Aunt May was rushed into hospital?'

'What? How is she? I swear I didn't know.'

Mike stared at him seeing the lie before Tony dropped his eyes, going along with it for the moment he said. 'Yeah, well, she was very poorly- so poorly she was in a coma, but thank God she's out of it now. According to Smiler, she came to just a few minutes after I left for London. Where the fuck were you? And why weren't you answering your phone?'

Tony sighed. 'I'll make arrangements to go up tonight.'

'You better, mate, or I'll want to know the reason why. Especially as, according to you, you have extended leave. In the mean time, you can tell me what I need to know, which is why you are mixed up with these freaks. And stop trying to change the subject. Remember, I saw you shoot that crazy bastard's double at the monastery.'

Sitting back down in his chair, Tony asked, 'Do you want a fresh drink?' He looked at his watch. 'Though there isn't much time. The old man in the bookshop has the place riddled with cameras from every angle possible, because the place is full of rare books. There's no getting away with it, Mike.'

'Make it go away.'

'I've already tried.'

'Try again, fucking harder.'

'Just go, Mike, now, while you can.' Tony stood up and went to a desk in the corner, He took a key from behind a picture of a magnificent wolf, peering back at the photographer from behind a tree, and opened a drawer. He dipped into the drawer, and pulled out a thick white envelope. 'Here, take this.' He handed the envelope to Mike.

With a suspicious look, Mike took the envelope. Opening it, he found it stuffed with money. 'Why?' he asked, frowning.

'I knew you would need it.'

'How? You reading minds now? Plus you haven't had time to get this sort of cash out of the bank.'

'Look, it's money I keep for emergencies, in case I have to make a quick getaway. Like you have tonight.'

'Why would you need to get away?'

Waiting for Tony's answer, Mike quickly scanned the room. Why didn't I realise before? It should have dawned on me, why he hardly ever asked me over here. No way could a copper afford this- unless he was a copper on the take. And the cash! By the thickness, there's gotta be a couple of grand at least.

Should have seen the signs a good while back.

He's been in with the bastards for years!

Tony's voice invaded his thoughts. 'Mike, just take the money and go. I'm trying to save your friggin' life here.'

'Are you? They don't hang people in England any more, Tony, didn't you know? Or is it a different organisation you're trying to save me from, and not the law?'

Tony rested his elbows on his knees, and put his chin on his hands. 'Just go.' He sighed. 'I'll be in touch, promise. Now! It's already nearly too late.'

Mike shook his head. So much he wanted to know, but he was over a barrel here. Tony was right. If he didn't run now, soon he wouldn't be able to run at all.

He headed for the door. Turning, he looked at Tony. For the brief moment that their eyes met, Mike recognised the torment staring back at him.

Again, he asked himself: just what the fuck is he involved in?

Knowing that he was not going to get anything out of him, Mike did the sensible thing, and got out as quickly as he could.

After Mike closed the door, Tony went to the window. He stood there for ten minutes, but there was no sign of Mike leaving the building. 'It's like he's disappeared into the night,' Tony muttered, a pleased smile on his face as he pulled the blinds down and hastily got on with his packing.

CHAPTER FORTY

Annya sat in the boot of the silver Range Rover. It was the only place for her. Thank God it wasn't a normal car, she thought, because she would have ended up in the boot of that as well, all crouched up, to finally emerge stiff and aching. She'd travelled that way before. At least here she could sit up, and even though it was dark, she could read the road signs and get an idea of where she was.

Lovilla sat in the front with her father, who loved to drive and rarely relinquished the wheel to another. In the back, two hench-men, both packing guns, relaxed. One of them was asleep -Annya could hear the soft rhythmic sound of his breathing. The other was looking out of the window.

She'd heard them talking earlier, both of them wondering why the meeting had been moved from London to Norwich. Shortly after, Lovilla had freaked out because she wanted the London shops. Annya had been on the receiving end of Lovilla's anger, and now had a black eye and a force-fed cover story to go with it, in case anyone asked how she had done it.

Classic. Walked into a door.

Ha! Like anyone's gonna believe that...

Escape at the moment seemed impossible, a fleeting dream. But she was still determined. Somehow, some way she would manage it, even supposing she died trying. She'd envisaged so many scenarios, and rejected them all, that her head hurt.

They pulled off the motorway and were soon in Norwich city centre. They drove straight through and out the other side. Annya stared at the people as they passed, longing to call out to them -but she knew that would be suicide.

Ten minutes later, they came to a stop outside a large country house. She guessed that it was a hotel, but a very exclusive one, as there were no signs on the road telling you it was here. Annya figured it would probably only take twenty or thirty minutes to run back to Norwich. If -I ever get the chance.

And where then?

Having been among the Families for a good time now, she knew their workings, and knew that finding someone to trust would be practically impossible - as impossible as trying to escape.

The jeep stopped outside of a double-door entrance. She had barely straightened up before the boot was lifted and a large hand was wrapped around her arm. She was dragged out, along with the suitcases. Not once did she feel his grip loosen.

'Smarten yourself up, girl,' he whispered in her ear, squeezing her right breast. 'Or you'll be dead before the morning comes. It won't take long to get a replacement for you. Two a penny, that's what you lot are.'

Annya quickly brushed her dress down, trying to get rid of the creases, pushed her hair behind her ears, and pulled a few locks over her black eye.

'Good,' he said. 'Now take these.' He threw her backpack at her, then handed her a small pink suitcase. 'Walk in front of me. Do not dare to veer off anywhere.'

Nodding, she quickly slipped the backpack onto her shoulders and picked up the suitcase.

She followed the other man, the one who had been asleep, up the seven stone steps and through the massive medieval double doors. Inside, the front hall was breathtaking. Never had she seen any place so magnificent. The smell was of old lavender polish, the same as her grandmother used to use back in the old country. It made her more homesick than ever.

A huge gold unicorn stood at the side of the staircase next to the desk, rearing so far above her head that she had to actually throw her head back to see its face. The carpets were red and luxurious, as if laid out for Hollywood stars to walk on. Seven huge chandeliers filled the large reception area with bright glittering light. It was all she could do to stop herself from saying a breath taken, 'Wow!' Without doubt, from what she knew of them, this was a Families stronghold. A gathering place for them all!

She had no chance of escape from here. How had she ever

thought that she would? Her heart sank. The others were depending on her, but it was impossible. She would be a prisoner for life. A breath caught in her throat with her next thought: however long that lasted.

She watched as Kirill Tarasov checked in, and actually flirted with the pretty blonde receptionist, then they all piled into a lift that took them to the second floor. She was squashed between both of the guards. The English one smirked at her until the lift doors opened. Lovilla took the key for room nineteen from her father and opened the door. The English guard followed them into the room with the suitcases. On the way out, he looked at Annya and used the universal gesture of pointing his forefinger and middle finger at his eyes, then pointing to hers. I will be watching you.

Annya shivered. Another breath caught in her throat as he closed the door behind him. She glanced at Lovilla, who had been watching. Her face held a smirk, as she said, 'Go to your room, peasant, you will not be needed tonight… Well, on second thoughts, I might find a use for you.'

Picking her backpack up. Annya quickly turned. There were two doors facing her. One was obviously hers, the other Lovilla's. She knew her choice would be met with scorn if she should choose the wrong one.

The decision was taken out of her hands a moment later when Lovilla snapped at her, 'Aren't you forgetting something, you stupid little peasant?'

Heart beating rapidly, Annya turned. She looked up from under her lids at Lovilla, terrified of what might be expected of her.

'The cases, fool! Surely to God you don't expect me to unpack them myself,' she said, a look of pure amazement on her face.

'Sorry, Miss.' Annya said quickly. Dropping her backpack and grabbing the nearest case, she headed for the bedrooms. Outside the doors, she hesitated.

'The one on the right! Oh, you are such a pathetic little peasant. Why do I put up with you?'

'Sorry, Miss,' Annya repeated as she opened the door. Quickly, she unpacked the case and hung everything in the wardrobe, then went back for the other one.

When she was finished, she quietly closed the door behind her, grabbed her backpack off the floor and stepped over to the next bedroom door. She was turning the handle, delivering up a thank you prayer and about to breathe easily, when Lovilla said, 'Would you like something to eat, peasant?'

Annya turned to see that room service had delivered while she'd been in the bedroom. Laid out on the table was more than enough food for a large family, at least half a dozen different dishes. It was then she noticed that the table was set for two.

Oh my God, she thought, her heart tripping. Just the very thought that Lovilla had ordered the table to be set for two was enough to give her an anxiety attack.

She needed time to breathe, time to figure out what to do.

What would Jaz do?

Go along with it, that's what she would do, just take it in her stride as usual.

That's how she's survived this long.

'I've…I need to g-go t-to the toilet,' she stammered. Running into her room and closing the door behind her, she ran to the bathroom, shut that door and slid the bolt.

That won't stop them, she thought, sitting on the toilet seat, staring at the flimsy bolt. Lovilla wouldn't even need one of the heavies to break that down. So fragile. A whisper, a breath would blow it down.

She looked around the small but luxurious bathroom, white tiles and solid gold fittings. Her eyes passed over the open window, then quickly skittered back.

She blinked. The window was wide open. Somehow she felt as if it was beckoning her towards it. Slowly she tiptoed over the luxurious red carpet, the few small steps that were needed to reach the window. Standing on her toes, she leaned out and carefully looked around. Two feet below the window was a thick ledge that ran the length of the building.

Go for it, she thought, excitement building in her body as she looked around again.

Without thinking how she was ever going to reach ground level, or even how she was going to get across the well-lit grounds to tree cover well over a hundred yards away, she climbed out of the window. She decided to go left, certain, even though it was gloomy, that she could see an old-fashioned fire escape at the end. Praying that's what it was, and with her back pressed against the building, she slowly edged, inch by trembling inch, along the ledge which was the exact width of her feet. Terrified to look down, she was praying the whole time that, although they were at the back of the place and it seemed deserted, no one would look up and see her.

She was halfway along now, concentrating so hard that she had no idea how much time had passed. She chewed her bottom lip, thinking, I'm never going to make it. No way.

Her calves were aching but, knowing that pain would be nothing to what they would put her through if they caught her up here, she moved on. She was just about to pass a window, which thankfully was in darkness, when she heard footsteps just below her. Heart beating rapidly, she squashed into the side of the window and kept perfectly still. Hearing what sounded like a dustbin lid being lifted and, a minute later, put back on, she held her breath until the footsteps retraced and went back into the building.

Taking a deep breath to calm herself, she wondered if she should maybe turn around to get past the window, which had a four-inch wooden sill on top of the ledge. It would be more than difficult doing it backwards. She could cling onto the top of the window, if she turned. It would be easier than what she was doing now.

'But how to get turned back round again?' she muttered.

You won't know until you try. She heard her grandfather's favourite saying in her head, and gained courage. She wanted to escape as much for him as she did for herself. For a moment, her eyes misted over, thinking of the torment he must be going through. Then she swung her leg onto the sill and moved on, every moment expecting Lovilla's head, or one of her guards', to pop out of the window and grab her.

She safely manoeuvred the turn after the window, although it seemed to take forever. Each minute she expected to miss her footing. At the end of the building, there was indeed a fire escape, old and rusted, and leaning into the wall as if they were melded together. It also looked like it had never been used before. But a fire escape was a fire escape, she thought, lifting her right leg and swinging her body round until she was facing the building again. A small step, and she was onto the fire escape, grabbing tight hold of the rail at each side.

For a moment it shook, making a loud groaning noise, and she thought it was going to come off the wall. As the noise ran all the way down to the bottom, she clung to the first rung, her heart speeding up. Thankfully, it held. All she really wanted to do now was go as fast as she could, hit the ground running and go for it, but the noise would have the whole building out wondering what was going on. Slowly, keeping herself in check, step by tortured step, she made her way down.

Wondering why Lovilla hadn't raised the alarm yet, she stared at what might be the biggest task yet- getting across the well-lit yard without being seen.

Make a bolt for it? she thought, looking up at the light, realising that she probably could have smashed it as she was passing. Then again, it could have been her undoing. One slip, and she would have been lying on the concrete, twisted up in a mess of arms and legs and probably dead.

Not quite believing that she had made it to the ground, she stood for a moment, picturing her grandfather's face when she finally made it home.

A moment later, she heard a door open. She gasped, and quickly hid between two large bins, shaking with fear and praying that whoever it was didn't plan on putting out the rubbish.

CHAPTER FORTY-ONE

Frowning, Lovilla picked at her prawn salad, disappointed that she couldn't find anything to complain about. She loved seeing the dismay on a peasant's face if they thought they were in trouble.

Her father treated them as pets. She'd actually seen him pat and fondle them as one would a cat or a dog. He even had his stupid favourites… Silly fool!

They are nothing but vermin. And have to be eradicated as such before there is nothing left on the planet.

Why can't he see that?

She lifted the silver lid from a large platter and raised her eyebrows. Half a dozen strawberry and custard tarts nestled together.

'Hmm,' she muttered. 'Who told them?' She wasn't really surprised, it happened everywhere she went. The peasants probably had a list of all the Families' favourite foods.

Feeling very pleased with herself, she sat back amongst the cream cushions and looked at the gold unicorns on the ceiling.

'Ha! Stupid peasants, you haven't got a clue what's coming. And neither, dear father, do you.'

Suddenly she sat up. 'Where the----?' Jumping off the bed, she ran to Annya's room. It took only a moment to see she wasn't there. Turning the handle on the bathroom door, she found it locked.

'Open the door. NOW.'

She rattled the handle, then put her shoulder to the door. The tiny bolt gave way with the first push. Angry Lovilla walked in, her eyes at once taking in the open window. This time she was truly amazed, perhaps for the first time in her life.

CHAPTER FORTY-TWO

Terrified even to breathe, Annya sat huddled in on herself. Then the footsteps stopped, she heard a click and guessed, rightly, that it was a cigarette lighter. She let out her breath and dropped her head onto her knees. A moment later, she jumped when she heard a voice from inside yelling, 'Get yourself back in here!'

'I've just flaming well lit up,' a man's voice yelled back, from only a few feet away.

'Get in here!' shouted the other voice, definitely a woman's, high pitched and squeaky.

'Oh, fucking hell,' the smoker yelled back. 'I am entitled to a break, you know.'

A loud harsh laugh was followed by, 'Not here you're not, mate. Remember? You sold your soul to this lot, you ain't entitled to nothing. Get used to it.'

A moment later, she heard the door closing. Without giving it any more thought, she jumped up and ran as fast as she could for the trees, every second expecting to be seen and the dogs set on her. Out of breath, she hid behind the first tree, before cautiously looking back at the hotel.

All quiet. Thank God, she thought as, still panting and trying to be as quiet as she could, she headed for the road.

God only knows what's creeping around in these trees. Beetles, worms, rats? She just managed to stifle a scream as she stood on something soft.

Oh help, please no.

Not a giant spider.

She shivered all over and, wanting to open her mouth and just scream her head off, she took another step.

'It's just dog's mess,' she muttered, trying to convince herself as she speeded up. 'That's all, or a fox's.' She froze for a brief moment. The thought of foxes on the loose terrified her even more. Shaking with fear she moved on, more slowly now, trying to be as quiet as she could.

Still got to get out of here. She prayed she was heading in the right direction. It was pitch black among the trees, and they seemed to be getting closer together.

Then she saw a faint patch between the trees which seemed slightly lighter. Turning more to her right, she headed towards it. She was nearly at the roadside when something touched her shoulder. She bit into her hand. The only thought in her head spider spider spider, she burst through the trees and jumped onto the road, and ran in a blind panic until she could run no more.

Slowing down, gasping, rubbing the stitch in her side, she

soldiered on.

'I'm going to make it, Grandpa, I'm coming home,' she repeated over and over. 'I'm coming home!'

A moment later her revived spirits hit rock bottom, when she saw the car in front of her. Black, with no lights on, it had been hard to see until it was close. Panicking, she looked quickly behind to see another car closing in on her.

It's them, she thought.

No way. She started to sob.

I am not going back there.

They can kill me before that happens.

The only option open to her was back into the woods, and pray she could find somewhere to hide. No way could she outrun them in the dark. They would know this place far better than she did.

Find some sticks, tree branches, anything to beat them off.

She looked around. Nothing, and there was no time to snap a branch off.

There must be somewhere to hide!

I can't give up now.

One of the cars had stopped within a few yards of her, and the one behind was catching up. The sound of the car doors being slammed spurred her on. She ran down the slight slope that led into the woods. Noise didn't matter any more, they knew where she was. If she could only make it out the other side before they caught her. She ran, crashing and weaving in case they had guns. She knew she was nothing to them. The only reason they wanted to catch her was to shut her up.

She made some progress, and began to hope that there was a chance, a tiny chance that she might even outrun them. The thought of freedom lured her on. From somewhere inside, she gained courage and a second wind.

Suddenly, she was grabbed from behind, then thrown roughly to the floor. She thrashed about, but her hands were quickly tied behind her back, a gag shoved into her mouth and a hood put over her head. She felt herself being lifted up and carried between two people.

All the fight she possessed deserted her. It didn't matter anymore. She had given up. She would never see her beloved grandfather ever again.

PART FIVE

CHAPTER FORTY-THREE

It wasn't the first time Mike had slept under the stars, although they were far more visible up home than they were in London. He was also convinced that the benches up home were much more comfortable. Probably being biased, he thought. After all, a bench is a bench, no matter where it is.

Not meaning to spend the night on the bench, he had merely sat down for a few minutes to sort his head out. The next minute he'd fallen fast asleep, and now his neck was stiff.

He stretched his neck to the left to get the kinks out, wondering how he'd gotten away with it. Amazing, really. He stretched his neck the other way.

Probably the last place they would think to look for a fugitive. Face it, though, that's what I am. He sighed. The idea did not sit well on his shoulders.

He knew he was filling his mind with random thoughts to stop thinking of Tony. They had become as annoying as a song stuck in your head that goes on and on.

He glanced at his watch. Seven o' clock, and the sun was just clawing its way up the sky. Leaving the park, he crossed the empty road to a small newsagent's shop. He looked at the news billboard before he went in, fully expecting his picture to be splashed under large headlines of his name.

Nothing! He frowned. Going inside, he picked up half a dozen newspapers. Nowhere was there any mention of a murder concerning him.

He bought a couple of the more well-known ones, then went back to the bench he now called home. He found nothing in the papers but celebrity sex lives, and phone hacking scams - until a small piece about CCTV cameras caught his eye. Every camera in London, at a certain time, had shown nothing but static. Strangely all the cameras in Norwich had done the same. The boffins had blamed sunspots.

'The lying bastards,' he muttered, when he saw the exact time the cameras had gone haywire.

He sighed as he threw the papers into a bin beside the bench. Tony knew all along that there was no CCTV of him, because the time they had all gone crazy was the same time as he had hit the guy in the bookshop. He'd wanted me out of the flat all along.

He must have been watching everything that happened, and come up with a story to get me out. Who the hell had he been expecting?

Frustrated and angry, Mike rose off the bench, ready this time to get everything out of Tony- no matter what it took.

He slipped quickly through a patch of trees towards the entrance of the park. Just as he was about to leave the tree cover, he spotted an old lady in a red coat. For a moment he stopped, then quickly moved further back.

'Well, talk about flaming coincidence. It's just gotta be the bird lady,' he muttered.

Best keep hidden, he thought, slipping further back, enough so that he could see and not be seen.

This is a good way from the police station, he thought, then realised that he didn't actually have a clue where she lived. Maybe she was heading to a tube station, to get into the heart of the city.

The path she was walking on was at least fifty yards away from where Mike was hiding, across a well trimmed grass area with more trees on the other side, which were much closer to the path. She'd only gone a few more steps when three youths, one black, the other two white, all wearing hoodie's covering their heads, slipped out from behind the trees.

They followed her for ten yards or so. It was clear what their intentions were. Then, for one split second, she paused, before spinning round and facing them. By now Mike was halfway across the grass and pulling his gun. He had no intention of using it, because there were no bullets in, just something to scare them off with, save using his fists on the pathetic scum.

Before he reached her, two were lying flat on their backs and the other was running for the trees.

'What the----?' Mike would have sworn that an old woman would never have been able to do what she did. Tucking his gun away, he said, 'You all right?'

Before answering, she kicked the nearest youth and said, 'On your way, scumbag.' Both boys jumped up, one nursing his jaw, the other favouring his right shin and limping, quickly they followed the path their friend had taken.

Unbelievable, Mike was thinking, as she turned to him and said, 'Nothing to worry about, Durham lad.'

CHAPTER FORTY-FOUR

The dawn light crept slowly into the hospital room. Danny sat staring into space. He hadn't moved from his chair since he got here. The machines that Evan was wired up to had constantly bleeped their way to morning. He sighed. He didn't know what was hurting the most, his head or his heart. He felt like screaming, the bleeping sound was more annoying than fingernails scraping on glass. He felt that all he had seen for days had been prison cells and hospitals.

Then he felt lousy for even feeling lousy. Nothing he had gone through could compete with what Evan was suffering, and would probably go on suffering.

He looked across at his friend, probably the only friend he had in the whole world right now. He was in a sort of cage, with the blankets lifted off his burned skin, which was more than 80% of his body. They said the next twenty-four hours would tell if he lived or died.

Danny was sure he'd heard one of the nurses whisper to the other that it would be kinder if he died.

Danny shivered. No way!

'Not Evan an' all,' he muttered, remembering them huddled by the doorway a few hours ago.

He'd wanted to yell at them, scream, rant and rave at the heavens, but instead he'd leaned over the bed, and whispered, 'You'll pull through, mate. I know you will.'

Now he wished he could touch him, to let him know that he was there for him. Reassure him that everything would be all right. But there was nowhere that wasn't burned apart from his back.

He needed to let him know that he would always be there for him, no matter what. It didn't matter what he looked like now, they could do marvels with plastic surgery these days.

'You'll be all right, Evan,' he said, remembering from somewhere that people in comas could sometimes still hear you. 'Don't worry, mate. I'll be here for you. We'll get through this together, mate.' He patted the side of the bed. He couldn't imagine life without Evan. They had been friends for so long, closer than a lot of brothers he knew.

His face was a few inches from Evan's when the machine flatlined. Jumping back in shock, Danny stared for a moment - then panic set in and he ran to the door. Before he reached it, the doctors and nurses were running in and pushing him out of the way.

Horrified, Danny stood and watched them. All of them donned special gloves, then went to work to resuscitate him. Danny cringed when they lifted the paddles off Evan's chest the first time, and scraps of thin skin were curled around them.

They tried again, and again to revive him, but there was no response. Evan wasn't there any more.

Evan's parents had gone out half an hour earlier for tea. They arrived back as the team were shaking their heads and switching his life support off. Evan's mother collapsed onto the floor.

Danny couldn't take his eyes off Evan.

How is it possible? he wondered, shaking his head in denial.

How can someone be a living, breathing human being one minute and not the next?

How?

Slowly, a broken man, he turned and walked out of the room.

CHAPTER FORTY-FIVE

Waking up, Smiler stretched - before quickly sitting up, a look of pure horror on his face.

His link to Mike had faded overnight, as if a strong rod of iron had become mist that could barely be seen.

Throwing the quilt back, he jumped out of bed. 'Gotta go, gotta find Rita, she'll know what's going on and why I can't find Mike,' he muttered.

He dressed quickly, his grey track suit with a new red t-shirt. He still had not got over the luxury of clean clothes every day. His skin revelled in the feel of the soft material.

Downstairs, everything was back in order. They had all worked for hours last night, he, Aunt May, Brother David, Jill and her girls. Aunt May had just put the phone down, and was sitting with an angry look on her face. There was no sign of Brother David. As Tiny was also missing, Smiler guessed that they were out walking.

'What's the matter?' he asked Aunt May.

'They've let him go.'

Smiler frowned. 'Who?'

'The bloody swine from the mainland, him who's been filling in at the shop. The bloody swine who trashed the place. Half an hour they had him for last night, that's all, bloody half an hour.'

Smiler pulled a face. He wasn't surprised. From what he had learned, the Families could do anything they wanted. He didn't know what to say to her, except, 'Well, he better not still be at the castle.'

'No. Kristina said he was picked up from the station and taken straight to Newcastle Airport.'

'Did the coppers say who he was? Does the regular guy really know him?'

Aunt May frowned. 'No, some sort of bloody agency worker. The real shop owner's a good guy, he'll not have known anything about this. But I have an idea.'

This flummoxed Smiler. 'What do you mean?'

'Never mind, son. You look like you have the weight of the whole bloody world on your shoulders.'

'I, em…I do have something to tell you.'

'Well, sit down and spit it out, lad. Though I have a bloody good idea what it is, an' all.'

Smiler stared at her for a moment before he sat down next to her. 'How…?'

'You're going after Mike.'

'How did you----? Never mind,' he sighed. 'I have to find him,

Aunt May. He's fading away.'

'Nowhere Man, eh?'

'Something like that.'

'OK.Take the Shetland pony.'

'What?'

'You heard.'

'But he'll get in the way.'

'No, he'll help protect you. There are some evil people out there, and that bloody dog adores you.'

'Does he?'

'Of course he does, you can see it in his eyes every time you come into the bloody room.'

Smiler sighed. 'Guess he does,' he said with a small smile.

Aunt May patted his hand. 'I've packed a haversack for you. Clean clothes, a bit of cash and a ticket to London to be picked up at the station.'

'How did----?'

She tapped the side of her nose with her forefinger. 'Let's just say it wasn't hard to figure out.'

CHAPTER FORTY-SIX

Shelly was sitting on a bench, underneath the trees at the bottom of Timber Hill, eating a bacon sandwich. It had rained earlier, but the sun had been up for over an hour and soaked up all traces, apart from a few damp spots under the trees. She watched the busy crowds bustling by and sighed, the weight of her knowledge pressing heavy on her heart.

Ordinary people passing by, that's all they are, without a clue as to how they are being manipulated.

Force-fed daily from TV and newspapers. Hidden instructions in every advert. Oh, God, it just goes on and on!

She looked at the half-eaten sandwich, her appetite all but gone. She was tempted to throw it in the bin, but knew she had to eat it.

Damned diabetes!

Bet they've got a cure for this hidden away. Bet none of them suffer from it, and that's a fact. Bastards.

She forced the rest of the sandwich down, even though it made her feel sick. Then she faced up to the real problem. She hadn't slept a wink last night. Murder, which was clearly what she had done, was most definitely not her thing.

Even though the swine deserved it.

Can I do it again, though? she wondered. And how many other girls have they done the same things to that they did to me? How many have they murdered?

They deserve to die.

The whole stinking lot of them.

Can I learn to live with the consequences, though?

She sat for a further half hour, torturing herself, one minute wanting to murder the whole lot, the next minute eaten up with guilt. Then pictures of Alicia entered her mind, Alicia laughing at old movies staring Jerry Lewis -Shelly had never heard of Jerry Lewis until Alicia introduced her to the movies- and Alicia crying because her pet cat Misty had died. The memories, flowing one after another, hurt. They also made her angry.

The thought of Alicia lying dead after how they had tortured her made her grind her teeth in anger.

Taking a deep breath and squaring her shoulders, she decided to carry on. Refusing to feel guilty any more, she was about to stand up when an old woman in a red coat sat down beside her.

'Nice morning,' the old woman said. 'Well, it is now, after all that rain we had through the night.' She smiled at Shelly as she took a bag of bird food out of her pocket, and threw a handful on to the ground. Within moments they were surrounded by pigeons greedily pecking at the corn.

'Talk about raining cats and dogs,' she went on. 'Jesus! Really set my arthritis off. Still feeling it now, even though the sun is cracking the pavements. I would love to live where the sun shines every day, wouldn't you? 'Cause them tablets the docs give you are rubbish. Don't even get near to the pain.' She rubbed her hands. 'Did you know----'

'Yes, yes, it is…a nice day,' Shelly interrupted her.

Really, really haven't got time for this, she thought, half rising from the bench.

'Planning any more murders for today?' the old woman asked, quite innocently, as if murder was an everyday thing and something you asked a stranger in polite conversation.

Dropping back onto the bench, Shelly gasped and nearly choked. 'What…what do you mean?' she managed a moment later, staring at the old woman, her face as red as the woman's coat.

'Well, you got away with yesterday's, didn't you, but only through luck…Trust me, it won't happen again. Normally insulin can't be detected, it's one of the last things they look for - but that lot's doctors are far in advance of any the National Health Service have.' She gave a short laugh. 'Much more advanced. And then there's the cameras. Oh yes, lots of CCTV footage, though apparently- and luckily for you- there was no CCTV footage in the whole of Norwich for a short time last night. That's probably the reason you're alive and enjoying the sun this morning.'

'Who...who the hell are you?' Shelly looked in amazement at the old woman.

'Someone you've been looking for.'

Shelly frowned as she slipped to the end of the seat. Getting ready to run, she put her right foot firmly on the ground.

Sensing this, the old woman said, 'Don't panic. I'm not one of the Families. I belong to the other group you've been looking for.'

'Oh, thank God.' Shelly wanted to cry as she sank back onto the bench. 'You are real.'

'About as real as you can get,' the woman replied with a smile.

'I wasn't a hundred per cent sure. So many rumours, sometimes it's hard to pick the fact from the fiction.'

The old woman nodded. 'You're safe now.'

Shelly was trembling inside. She couldn't believe her luck. They had found her. 'So, what now?'

'Now you come with me, Shelly.'

CHAPTER FORTY-SEVEN

Kirill Tarasov glared at his daughter, who defiantly glared right back at him. Before he could launch into a tirade, Lovilla shouted, 'How was I to know she would climb out of the fucking window? Stupid peasant. You can't blame me.'

'You don't understand,' Tarasov growled. 'She still has not been found. Have you any idea at all what sort of trouble can escalate from this?' he loomed threateningly over her.

But Lovilla stood her ground. 'Where were the fucking guards then, eh? Where were they? How can one fucking skinny little peasant escape from us?'

'It's not the first time,' Tarasov snapped.

Lovilla stamped across the floor towards the door, then spinning round moved back until she was within a foot of her father. 'Where were the guards?' she demanded again, in his face. 'Shoot the bastards.' Realising she may have gone too far in confronting him so closely, she retreated a few steps.

'It's the guards fault,' she repeated, folding her arms across her chest. 'And how the hell have they not found her, with all the resources we have? It's impossible.'

'They're still poring over the satellite pictures. For some strange reason, on a clear night, there was a lot of static.' He frowned. 'Almost as if there was deliberate interference.'

'Impossible.'

'I would have said the same a few years back, but some odd things have been happening lately. That's why the meeting has been changed from London to here. That was before they found out that the satellite interference only covered the Norwich and London areas. Everyone has been asked to attend, that's why your brother is on the next flight.'

'Do you think that the fool's guard may have been murdered?' Lovilla asked, changing the conversation away from herself.

'Yes, I do. Although nothing really shows up on that hotel screen, and the interference lasts for only a minute or so, I'm quite sure there is someone else in the picture as he got out of the car.'

'What's he doing in Norwich, anyhow, knowing there's a price on his head? The fool.'

'And that's exactly what he is, a fool. From what I've heard, he's going to make an entrance at the meeting and demand that he be restored to full Family membership.'

Lovilla crossed the room and picked up her cigarettes and lighter from a small round table near the door, her silver-painted nails glinting in the sunlight. 'Do you honestly think it will happen?' she asked, lighting a cigarette and aroggantly blowing smoke towards her father.

He scowled and wafted his hands at the smoke. 'Oh, yes, in some respects he's indispensable.'

'To you, maybe.'

'And you, too, daughter. His services keep us from hunting our own meat. Remember that.'

Scowling, Lovilla changed the subject again. 'It has to be them,' she said with conviction. 'The bastards have been a thorn in our sides for generations. Somehow, they must have rescued the fucking peasant. It was probably all planned.'

Tarasov clicked his tongue. 'They call themselves the Descendants of Boudicca. Just a bunch of silly women with nothing better to do. How could they plan anything remotely like this? Satellite interference? I doubt it.'

'Ha! If they're just a bunch of silly women, how come they've managed to outwit us all these centuries? How come their dead patron managed to kill all those Romans, eh?'

'You think too much.' He turned and strode out.

CHAPTER FORTY-EIGHT

Having finished breakfast and helped Coral to wash the dishes, Annya was revelling in her freedom. No one ordering her about. No jangled nerves, wondering what was going to happen in the next five minutes. Last night had seemed as if she was in a dream - to finally feel safe and to know she had outwitted the Families, it had been fantastic. And then they had explained to her that she would never truly be free until it was all over. That perhaps it wasn't even safe to let her grandfather know that she was still alive.

Now Coral was sitting with her, in the large conservatory attached to the house where Annya had been brought last night. The dozen or so windows each held a plant pot filled with blooming orchids, alternately arranged in pink and white. She revelled in the fact that she was wearing jeans and a yellow t-shirt, which had been given to her by Coral. She wouldn't have chosen the t-shirt herself - far too revealing, very low frontage as well as hanging off her right shoulder. But she was grateful. Anything was better than the blue sack things she'd been forced to wear.

Coral had filled a few things in for her about exactly who

they were, and what they were doing against the might of the Families. What they had done over the centuries.

Overawed by their accomplishments over the years, Annya was smiling for the first time in months. Then the door opened, and an old woman in a red coat walked in, followed by someone she knew. Annya gasped.

Shelly, who had also had a smile on her face, froze when she recognised Annya.

Oh, God, she thought. Annya was one of the girls that she herself had recruited. She remembered the time and the place. She had lured Annya round one of the back streets in Newcastle with the promise of cheap Justin Bieber downloads. The van had already been waiting. She'd even helped hold her until the chloroform worked.

She'll hate me -and I don't blame her.

What to do?

Just turn and walk away.

Then what?

Carry on the way she had been, until they caught her and did what they had done to Alicia?

She knew, though, that she had to face up to it. She'd done what the Leader had ordered, not only out of fear, but to keep herself in the little yellow pills that she still had a craving for every time she thought of them.

I've still got the gun in my bag. Perhaps I should use it now, end it all, over and done with, no more fear, no more shame.

No more hiding!

The option of ending it all was becoming sweeter by the moment.

First, she felt as if she should throw herself at Annya's feet and beg her forgiveness- although she knew what she herself would have done, if Alicia had begged her for forgiveness. Darling, sweet Alicia had had another side to her, that neither Evan nor Danny had known about. Suddenly, sanctuary didn't look so good. Not with the constant reminder that was Annya, staring her in the face every morning.

Lowering her eyes, she stared at the blue and green rug.

Ella walked past her into the middle of the conservatory and started taking her clothes off. She rid herself of the red coat first, then the wig and face-mask, revealing a pretty, brown-haired young woman underneath it all. Both Annya and Shelly gasped in surprise as they stared at her.

'Well done, Ella,' Coral said.

Ella grinned. 'Shelly, meet Annya and Coral. Annya, meet Shelly.'

'We've already met,' Shelly mumbled.

Ella looked quickly round at Annya, whose face was chalk white as she stared at Shelly.

Guessing the truth, Coral said, 'Oh- you both come from Newcastle way, don't you.' She sighed. 'Guess I know what's happened here, then.'

Shelly nodded. 'I'm sorry, truly, truly sorry… Please believe me.'

Annya turned away and stared out of the window as Coral, getting up out of her seat, gestured with her head at Ella that the two of them should leave.

When they had gone, Shelly moved closer to Annya, and said again, 'I'm sorry, Annya, truly I am.'

'Go away,' Annya replied, still refusing to look at her.

'But you don't understand. The same was done to me by a very good friend.'

'And that makes it all right for you to do it to me, does it? Just because you were addicted to the stupid drugs? Well, so was I. I spent God knows how many weeks in a forced hell trying to come off them. Have you any idea what it's like?'

'Yes.'

'Is that it? "Yes"?'

'No… Yes… Look, I know it doesn't make it right, but I am sorry. Please tell me what I can do to make it right. I'll do anything, anything at all.'

Annya finally turned and faced her. 'Nothing. There is nothing you can do.' Her voice rising with every word, she went on, 'Go away. I hate you. Hate you for what you did to me, for what you put me through. For what you put my grandfather through, and for what he's still suffering.'

'I… I'm sorry.'

'Sorry isn't good enough, nor will it ever be. You have ruined my life. How many others?' she demanded.

'I don't know.' Shelly hung her head. She couldn't stay here. It was obvious that Annya would never forgive her for what she'd done. She thought of the rows she'd had with Alicia, unknown to Evan and Danny, about pretty much the same thing.

And she thought of the gun in her bag.

CHAPTER FORTY-NINE

'Never saw that one coming, did we?' Coral said, as she and Ella walked down the garden path. The path was edged with flowers, and lawned on both sides, with a small pond full of fat golden fish at the bottom. The fish belonged to Ella, who had names for them all. Each was called after one of the seven dwarves. Grumpy had recently died, and Coral had begun to think that Ella was never going to snap out of it- though secretly she suspected that Ella was using the death of her pet as an excuse to delve into a little self-pity. Not that anyone could blame her, really.

Ella had been rescued over five years ago. Her story at the hands of the Families was horrendous. It had taken over a year for her to step outside the safe house, and the fact that she could not contact her two children, for their own safety, ate away at her on a daily basis. They were still being watched, as were the family members of everyone involved. Except for those, like herself, who had managed to fake their own death.

A six foot high fence encircled the property, keeping them safe from prying eyes. Ella sat down on one of the green striped deckchairs beside the pond. Coral took the red striped one facing Ella, and lit up a cigarette.

'Hmm. It's not going to be easy with both of them in the same house, is it? Remember, Louise had a similar situation at the safe house in London.'

'Yes,' Coral nodded. 'When one of the girls lost it, and used a knife on the other.'

'We mustn't ever forget what these girls have been through. At the end of the day, we've been there as well. It's our job to ease them back, the best way we can. After all, it's been going on for a hell of a long time.'

Coral sighed. 'I think we'd better put Shelly on suicide watch. She does have that gun with her. Big mistake. I should have taken it away last night. But I thought she needed it for comfort, and would lose trust if she thought we could more or less do what we wanted with her.'

'Do you think she's the type to kill herself?'

'Is there truly a type?'

Ella shrugged. 'Best get that gun off her, then, in case that argument turns nasty. Annya seems a nice enough kid, but I don't think she's a pushover, by any means. It took a lot of guts to escape the way she did.'

Coral was about to reply when her phone rang. Looking at the caller ID, she said to Ella, 'It's Louise.'

Ella nodded. 'Good.' She waited patiently until Coral put her phone back in her pocket.

'Everything's all right down there. She's made contact with a rather bemused Mike Yorke.'

Ella burst out laughing, and Coral joined her. A moment later, the sound of a single gunshot sent them running towards the conservatory.

CHAPTER FIFTY

Bored stiff from the long train journey - a fifty-five minute hold-up at York, plus a couple hell bent on kicking the shit out of each other who were put off at Peterborough, a further fifteen minute delay- and anxious to find Rita, Smiler finally arrived at Kings Cross station, his link to Mike no stronger than it had been in Northumberland. That added considerably to Smiler's worries. He'd strongly believed the closer to London he got, the stronger the link would get. To Smiler it felt as if he was missing a limb or two.

He and Tiny headed out of the station and crossed the road to MacDonald's. He tied Tiny up outside, and a few minutes later came out of the shop with a king size burger each for him and the dog. When Tiny had wolfed his burger down, and Smiler was still on with his, they headed along the street in the direction that Smiler knew he would find Rita.

Only Rita had gone very quiet, which was unusual. She was almost as quiet as Mike.

Smiler reached the place where Rita usually hung about, but there was no sign of her. He asked a couple of young boys who were standing down by the river throwing stones, but they hadn't seen her for a few days. In fact, no one had seen her.

He strolled along the path wondering what to do, because he didn't have the slightest idea where Rita lived. After about a hundred yards, he stopped for a moment and gazed at the river. Sitting down, he leaned back on his arms, the palms of his hands taking his weight.

Where the hell are you? he wondered.

'I'm here.'

Smiler shot up and looked around. Strutting towards him, on the highest pair of heels he'd ever seen, wearing a huge grin and very little else, a black leather mini skirt barely covering the top of her legs, and a pink blouse showing even more smooth flesh, was Rita. She waved at him.

'Where've you been?' Smiler asked, when she reached him.

Knowing that he did not mean where had she physically been, Rita answered, 'Sorry, love. Sometimes it happens for no reason. As long as you can feel me, I'm all right.'

'So Mike's----?'

'For the moment.'

As smooth and graceful as any young woman who had been to a top finishing school, Rita sat down on the grass. Smiling, she said, 'How's Aunt May?'

'You know her?' Smiler asked, his jaw hanging open in amazement.

'Oh yes. I also knew your mother.'

Smiler nearly choked in shock. 'How? How?' he gasped.

Rita rose as quickly and as gracefully as she'd sat down. Holding out her hand to Smiler, she said, 'Come on. We have quite a lot to talk about.'

Smiler looked at Rita's hand for a moment, at her long slim fingers, then reached up with his own. Quickly she pulled him to his feet.

CHAPTER FIFTY-ONE

Ella and Coral burst into the conservatory to see Shelly sitting on the floor, her head in her hands, and Annya holding the gun. For a moment they all froze.

Coral was the first to regain her wits. 'Put the gun down, Annya. Please,' she said calmly, as she took a step forward. 'While we check on Shelly.'

Obviously in shock, Annya stared at her. Coral held out her hand. 'Pass the gun over, Annya, please, and we'll sort it out. Shelly needs our help.'

Annya was shaking as she said, 'You think...you think I've shot her, don't you?' She looked accusingly at them.

'Tell me what happened.'

'She…she...' Annya started to cry and put her free hand over her face, her gun hand hanging slack with the gun pointing towards the floor. Using the opportunity, Coral reached Annya, preparing to wrestle her for the gun, but Annya lifted it up and handed it over. Fearing what she might find, Ella hurried to Shelly.

'She was going to shoot herself,' Annya said.

Coral breathed deeply. Taking the gun from Annya, she put her arms around the trembling girl's shoulders. Seeing no signs of any injury, Ella did the same to Shelly, who sobbed her heart out on Ella's shoulder.

'I'm sorry…I'm so sorry.'

'It's all right, Shelly. You've been through so much, I suppose something was going to give.' She lifted Shelly's chin and looked into her eyes. The misery lodged there made her want to cry. Instead, she said, 'It's OK, Shelly, you're safe now. Come on, I'll take you to your room and give you something to settle you down.'

Carefully, she helped Shelly off the floor. Leaning heavily on her, Shelly, in a daze, did what Ella said. A few minutes later Ella had Shelly undressed and in bed.

Downstairs, Coral puffed out her cheeks and said, 'It seems you've been very brave, Annya.'

Annya licked her dry lips and said, 'She just pulled the gun out of her bag. I thought she was going to shoot me'- she shivered- 'but she wasn't, she was going to kill herself.' She started to cry again.

'Come on, sit down,' Coral urged her.

Annya sat. Resting her elbows on her knees, dropping her head into her hands, staring at the floor, she said, 'We were arguing. I blamed her for what happened to me… I'm sorry, I never expected her to do what she did.'

'It's not your fault, Annya. No one can blame you for being

angry.'

'I know, but… She's been through so much herself.'

'A lot of us have.'

Annya looked at Coral. 'You too?'

'Yes. I'm afraid all of us here have our own tales to tell about what we suffered at the hands of those'- she paused for a moment, reflecting briefly on her own story - 'can't even bring myself to call them human beings.'

'And you all escaped?'

'With a little help. You don't think that bathroom window opened itself, do you?'

'You?'

'No, it was Ella, She has a part time job in there, sort of our woman on the inside. Of course, she couldn't make it too obvious, in case she herself was caught. No written evidence, nor any attempt to speak to you- she hoped by opening it as far as she could you might take the hint.'

'She's so brave, working amongst them.'

'It's our job, Annya, the way we fight back by rescuing as many as we can. Obviously we have to think of our own safety- if one of us gets caught, they'll torture us until they find out who is behind us. So we can basically only leave a hint or two, hoping who ever we try to rescue picks up on it. Hence, in your case, the wide-open window. Thank God it worked.'

'Who is behind all of this?' For a moment, Annya was worried. Were these the same sort of people as the Families? Were they rescuing people only to sell them on?

Ella arrived, carrying a tray with three cups of tea. Smiling, she put it down on the table.

Coral turned to her and said, 'Annya is wanting the whole story, Ella.'

Handing Annya a cup of tea, Ella said, 'I can only ask you to be patient for a few more hours, Annya. We will explain everything to you and Shelly, although she already has an idea. Just please trust us. You are safe here.'

CHAPTER FIFTY-TWO

Looking very dishevelled, in desperate need of a shave, Danny sat on a bench underneath a bright blue and yellow striped umbrella outside the local pub, nursing his fifth pint of beer in the last hour. He had come out for shopping, but judging by the look he got from the owner of the corner shop as he'd stepped through the door, he was far from welcome.

Deciding not to bother -it isn't worth the hassle, he'd thought at the time, the whole flaming world thinks I'm guilty- he'd headed for the local supermarket, where he'd prayed he might not be recognised. Then he'd passed the pub just as the doors were opening, and all thoughts of food flew right out of his mind.

But the hair of the dog idea proved to be a lie. He felt as lousy as he had when he'd woken up, after downing a full bottle of vodka last night. Might as well drink the lot, he'd thought at the time, no fucker else to share it with.

That had been over thirteen hours ago. He'd failed to make it to the bedroom, and had collapsed on the floor-he was now out and about in the clothes he'd fallen asleep in.

Staring into the dregs of his pint, he thought, Might as well get another. Nowt else to do.

Unsteadily, he got up from the bench and weaved his way into the dimly lit bar.

'Pint,' he slurred, digging his change out of his pocket.

'Not think you've had enough, lad?' asked the barman, a large man with a liking for green tartan shirts and long whiskery side-boards.

'No… What's yer problem, like, mate? My money not good enough for yer?'

'We don't want any trouble in here.'

'Not givin' yer any, am I? Just want me pint.'

'OK, OK. Just saying.' Keeping a steady eye on Danny, the barman poured the pint and put it on the bar, counted out the price from the change Danny had slapped down, and pushed the rest towards him.

Danny pocketed the change, looked at the barman and said, 'It's not fair, is it?'

Praying for the bar to fill up so he wasn't stuck listening to this guy's problems, the barman replied, 'There ain't nothing fair in this life, mate, nothing at all.' He moved along to the end of the bar and began dusting the fittings.

Danny mulled this over with a frown. 'So you're saying my life's as good as yours, eh?'

The barman ignored him.

'You ain't got any idea. You don't know what's fucking coming to you, mate, and that's a fact.'

'Is that a threat?' The barman put his duster down and moved towards Danny.

'Not off me, no way.'

'Then who?'

'Them,' Danny leaned over the bar and whispered. 'That's who. They're all over the place.'

Not another nutter, the barman thought, shaking his head and turning to move back along the bar.

Danny grabbed his sleeve. 'Them,' he said, this time in a loud stage whisper.

'I wouldn't do that if I were you.' The barman looked pointedly at Danny's hand on his arm.

Letting go, Danny sighed. He picked up his pint and, taking a large drink, he ran his tongue round his lips and went on, 'Well, don't say I didn't warn you. Better lock this place up and go away If I were you like, 'cause it's coming.'

'Why?' The barman could have kicked himself. He knew better than to encourage doomsday idiots like this. In his profession he'd heard them all.

'Just 'cause it is, and just 'cause they can.'

'Yeah, right.'

'It's a waste of time talking to people like you, isn't it? Never listen or see just what's under yer fucking nose. Give me a bottle of vodka.' Danny put a twenty-pound note on the bar.

'Taking it with you?' the barman asked hopefully.

'Aye,' Danny muttered, downing the rest of his pint.

Bottle of vodka tucked under his arm, Danny left the pub, his relationship with the barman intact, but only just. He decided to sit back down on the bench and have a drink of the vodka. Putting the bottle to his mouth, he slurped a good quarter of the bottle, barely stopping for air.

He was still there a good hour later, much to the barman's disappointment. He'd watched half a dozen people sit down and, after a few minutes of Danny's blurred ranting about doomsday, get up and leave.

Danny tipped the empty bottle upside down, catching a few drops with his finger. Then he put his finger in his mouth and sucked. Better go home, he thought, trying to stand up, a task he found rather hard as his knees wobbled every time he put some weight on them.

Giggling, he tried again. This time he managed to haul himself around the table, but succeeded in knocking the bottle onto the floor. He stared at the broken glass, and found it quite amusing as he wandered off. He laughed all the way to the main road. Then, face twisted into a scowl, he glared at the heavy traffic.

'Bring it on,' he muttered, stepping onto the road.

He was beeped at by a white van amidst a squeal of brakes, and the driver swearing loudly at him. Sticking his middle finger up, he stumbled further into the road. A car coming from the opposite direction spotted him just in time. Ignoring all the angry yelling directed at him from both sides of the road, Danny safely made it to the path, and headed for a narrow back street which cut his journey home by a good ten minutes.

CHAPTER FIFTY-THREE

Dreading what Rita had to tell him, and not quite certain that he really wanted to know, Smiler followed her into a large house in a quiet, leafy part of London, well away from her usual haunts. She showed him into the large sitting room which, knowing how flamboyant Rita was, surprised him - very plain with cream walls, where quite a few pictures of smiling people (mostly young girls) were scattered, a brown leather sofa and two matching arm chairs, and a love seat in the window, which was what Smiler headed for. He liked to be able to see outside so that no surprises were sprung on him.

'I won't be long,' Rita said, ruffling the thick hair on Tiny's neck. 'Gotta get out of these shoes right now, Smiler, my fucking corns are killing me.'

Smiler shrugged. 'Shouldn't wear them so high, then. It's not like you really need to.'

With a grin, Rita headed for the stairs. Here there were more cream walls, this time all bare until you reached the landing where you were faced with a huge picture of Rita at her finest. Blonde hair piled high on the top of her head, she was wearing a glittering silver and green ball gown, with a slit at the side, and striking a Marilyn Monroe pose.

Feeling thirsty, Smiler headed towards the kitchen for a drink of water. Cream again, only with a lot of blue added. It was a good sized kitchen, with a pine breakfast table. A door to the back garden was by the sink, with another door set further back.

Filling a blue mug with water from the tap, he was about to take a sip when he heard a noise. Frowning, he looked around. He could have sworn he heard someone moaning. A moment later, the moans came again. It sounded as if pretty soon the moaning could turn to screaming.

Wonder if someone's fallen down?

Rita never said she lived with anyone, but this house is massive, plenty big enough for six or seven people. He hesitated. Really, it's not my place, whoever it is might tell me to piss off… But they might need help. Might even be dying. Oh shit! Gently he knocked on the door in the corner. 'Can I help?'

He waited, his ear pressed to the door, before asking again if he could help, only to be answered with more moaning. He looked at the round knob on the door. Should I? he wondered.

'What the hell. They might need help, and Rita's taking some flaming time up there,' he muttered, turning the knob.

Inside it was very dim, because of the dark blue blind pulled down over the window. He waited for a moment for his eyes to adjust. When they did, he saw a young girl lying on a bed, curled up on herself, in the throes of misery. She suddenly started thrashing about. Then the screams came, low and slow at first, before building up to an ear splitting climax.

Smiler hurried into the room and, reaching the bed, took hold of her hand, understanding exactly what was wrong with her and knowing there was very little he could do except be there for her. She seemed to glean a small comfort from his presence, and kept tight hold of his hand. She even began to quieten down. A few minutes later, Smiler was not surprised to hear Rita behind him.

'She's going cold turkey. Her choice. Sadly, the methadone was a complete waste of time. Her name's Lynne. Tiny little thing, isn't she? We've had her for five and a half weeks now. God bless her, she's determined to beat it. Like I said, the methadone didn't work- but you'll know all about that.'

Nodding sadly, Smiler turned, and got a shock. Instead of Rita standing there, it was a man.

'Hello.' He held out his hand. 'I'm Robert.'

Smiler looked Robert up and down. If he hadn't heard him speak, he would never have guessed it was Rita's alter ego. Where Rita always wore a blonde wig, Robert was quite dark, and very handsome. Slightly bemused, although he knew it was bound to happen some time, Smiler held out his hand and they shook.

'Louise will tell you more about her when she gets back from her stint as the bird woman.'

'B-bird woman?' Smiler's jaw hung open. 'You mean the woman in the red coat, who stands outside the cop shop?'

'That's the one.'

CHAPTER FIFTY-FOUR

'OK, so that's a fiver each way on Sugar Rose in the 3.30 tomorrow?' Aunt May nodded as the bookie confirmed her bet. 'Thanks, son, be in on Friday to collect.'

'You're a witch, May. Pretty soon you'll have me bankrupt. Actually, might bang a fiver on it myself. See you Friday.'

She laughed out loud at his response. 'You do that, Frankie. Bye now.'

She put the phone down as Brother David came in from the kitchen carrying two mugs of tea.

'You still gambling, Aunt May?'

'Took a bloody gamble on you three, didn't I?'

Brother David smiled. 'I guess you did.'

Patting his hand after he put her tea on the table next to her, she said, 'And it bloody well paid off an' all… Erm -why don't you go and change into something more comfortable? I'm sure there's some joggers and t-shirts belonging to Mike upstairs that might fit you. Be a tight squeeze, but...' She shrugged.

'Does the robe make you uncomfortable, Aunt May?' Brother

David frowned.

'No, just thinking of your bloody comfort, that's all.'

'Or could you possibly be trying anything to put off the inevitable questions you know are coming?'

She shrugged. 'Fire away.'

He sat down facing her. 'OK, Aunt May, will do. Why here? Why would someone come in and wreck the place? And what are they looking for?'

'That's three bloody questions.'

'Answer them in whichever order you choose, my dear, but today I want to know what's really going on. Because some of the things that've happened are rather on the strange side… And just what do you have to do with it?'

She smiled. 'Where to start?' Brother David refused to react to her question. Instead he just smiled right back her.

'OK. It's a long story, going back many thousands of years.' She studied his face, but he showed no reaction. Instead he seemed quite calm, and determined to hear her out.

She sighed, having known that this day was inevitable. Too much had gone on, too much was going on, for those closest to her not to wonder. 'OK. Let's suppose that a long time ago, a group of very influential men got together and declared themselves, unknown to everyone else, of course, the rulers of the earth. It was theirs to do with, whatever they bloody well wanted. And that's exactly what they did, changing the course of human history time and time again. All for greed, all for profit. The descendants of those men are still here today, still secretly ruling us. They don't have a fancy name like you read about in all those bloody conspiracy theories. Give us quite a laugh, some of them, although others have amazingly come very close to the bone.'

'It doesn't sound so fanciful when you take a moment or two to think about it.' Brother David drank the rest of his tea, made him self more comfortable and nodded for her to go on.

She had just opened her mouth to speak when Jill knocked on the door and came in.

'Hi, Jill,' Aunt May said.

'Just popped in to see if you guys wanted anything at the shop? Thought I'd save you a trip over.'

'We're fine, Jill, thanks. I got what we needed this morning,' Brother David said.

'Cup of tea, Jill?" Aunt May asked.

'Yeah, why not.' Jill smiled at Brother David, who rose and went to freshen the pot.

Before sitting down, Jill said, 'Mind if I use your loo, May? Been running round all morning,'

'Of course, you know where it is.'

'Cheers.' Jill headed for the stairs. Behind her, the welcoming smile dropped from Aunt May's mouth. Noticing this on his way back in from the kitchen, Brother David put the fresh cup down and looked quizzically at Aunt May.

'We'll talk later,' she whispered quietly. 'Walls have bloody ears. We have to be very careful.'

Puzzled, Brother David said, 'All right.' He tried to rid himself of the mental picture of huge ears sprouting out of all the walls in the house.

Upstairs, Jill quickly opened the first of the six doors in the corridor. She knew one of them was Aunt May's room, but which one? This was obviously a kid's room, probably for some of her guests. The second door she guessed, because of all the flowers scattered on the walls and the curtains, must be Aunt May's. Quickly she went inside.

She hurried over and looked through the drawers, looking for, perhaps, a small key to a cupboard, she didn't really know. Something book-shaped. Finding nothing, she tried the wardrobe. The floor held quite a few pairs of shoes. Quickly she rummaged amongst them, testing the floor for a false bottom but came up with nothing. There was a door next to the wardrobe. Opening it, she found a bathroom. Won't be in here, she thought. Frustrated, and knowing she'd probably been too long, she hurried out of the room.

Downstairs, she rubbed her stomach as she walked into the sitting room and pulled a face.

'Not feeling too well?' Aunt May asked, with just the right tone of concern in her voice.

'Not really, May. Some sort of tummy bug, I guess. Think the girls are coming down with it, too.'

'There's one or two bugs doing the rounds,' Brother David said sympathetically.

Jill nodded. 'Perhaps I'd better leave the tea and get back home, May, I do feel a bit sickly. And I wouldn't want to pass it on. Perhaps a lie down.' She sighed. 'I do so hate to be ill.'

'It's OK, love. You have a good night's sleep tonight, and you'll feel better tomorrow.'

'Right. Bye, Brother David- don't get up, I'll see myself out.' She headed quickly for the door. Brother David, who had half-risen, dropped back into his chair.

'Bloody amateur,' Aunt May said. When she heard the door close behind Jill.

'What?'

'You heard.'

'Just what is going on here, Aunt May? Are you trying to say that Jill has something to do with all this?'

'She's one of them. One of the Families. In fact, she's a blood relative of the Leader.'

'What?'

'Yes, the man who enslaved you all.'

'But her daughter was in the monastery!'

'Yes, but he would have had no idea who she was. And if he had, he wouldn't have cared less. In fact, he would probably have got a kick out of it. He's an outcast, remember.'

'But didn't Jill think she might have been there?'

'Maybe, I don't know. There are hundreds of reasons teenagers take off. If Jill thought she was in there, trust me, she kept it bloody well hidden. To be honest, though, I don't even think she knew about the monastery. Her job was simply to befriend me, and find out what I knew about the missing book.'

'I can't believe you knew this.' He rose and began pacing the room. Three times he reached the door to the kitchen, turned and stared at Aunt May. Finally, he said, 'I don't believe it. No way can I believe that you knew what was going on and did nothing.'

'Don't you think I wanted to? But it was only weeks ago that I even found out about the monastery, right under my bloody nose an' all. We were planning something.'

Brother David frowned, wondering who she meant when she'd said we.

Before he could ask her, she went on, 'Remember the last I'd heard from you was that you were going on a long sabbatical. So for a good few months I wasn't worried. When I did find out, there was nothing I could do. This battle has been going on for centuries. I couldn't let the sisterhood be compromised.'

'The sisterhood?'

She sighed. 'You need to know a lot more before we even go there. For the moment, I will tell you what Jill was looking for, and what the bloody creep who wrecked the place was looking for. The Lindisfarne Gospels.'

'But isn't that in London?'

'A lot of people think it is, but as Keeper of the Book, I can tell you it bloody well isn't.'

'Keeper of the Book?' Brother David said. Slightly amazed, he repeated it again. He could barely believe what he was hearing. It sounded like the biggest conspiracy theory in the world. If he hadn't been part of it for a year in the monastery, he would have laughed at the thought of Aunt May being involved in anything remotely like this.

'An old title that I inherited,' Aunt May said.

'So…you have the book here?'

'Sorry, love, can't tell you.'

'What's in the book? Can you at least tell me that, seeing as it nearly cost your life?'

'The book contains the names of the Families, past and present. They have been searching for it for centuries. The last thing they want is for it to fall into the hands of the public.'

'So tell me, Aunt May -why haven't you exposed them before now? Really, dear, I find it impossible to believe that you----' He shook his head, unable to go on.

'We've never been bloody strong enough, that's why. They control the media worldwide, and some of the armies.'

'What?'

'Oh, yes. You name it, they have a big fat bloody finger in it. Trust me on that.'

Brother David shook his head. 'And you've kept this secret

for all this time?'

'Part of the job, son. They know about us, have done for a bloody long time. They've tried to ferret us out, but we've managed to keep one step ahead. Nearly got rid of us in that huge witch hunt a few centuries back. And in the time of Boudicca- now, she gave them bloody hell all right!'

'And Jill?'

'Jill is actually nothing more than a piece on a chess- board. She tried to walk away a good long time ago, but the Families don't let anyone go. She's only working for them out of fear, not loyalty. That's the reason she's so on edge all the time. I actually feel quite sorry for the poor girl.'

'OK, Aunt May, more tea and some sandwiches, then you can carry on filling me in on this'- he shrugged as if he only half-believed - 'this fantastical tale.'

Aunt May smiled. If only he knew, she thought.

CHAPTER FIFTY-FIVE

Danny woke up stiff and freezing, four hours after he'd fallen asleep on the kitchen floor. His mouth felt as if a rat had curled up and died in there, and the side of his face was nearly stuck to the floor with dribble and snot.

'Damn,' he muttered. Shivering, he used the table to haul himself up. Stretching, he went to the kitchen sink, where he splashed handfuls of cold water over his face before sticking his head under the tap. Surfacing a few minutes later, he dried himself off and, feeling only marginally better, began to look through the cupboards for a bottle of anything.

'Damn,' he said again, slamming the last door so hard that it shook just about everything in the flat. 'Gonna have to go out and get some shopping. Fuck the lot of them.'

He went into the bedroom. Stripping off his wet t-shirt, he threw it into a corner and found a clean one at the bottom of the drawer. It was pale blue and had Kiss me quick! printed on it. Danny stared at it trying to get the memory back, he knew it was probably more than ten years old. But couldn't remember buying it.

'Couldn't give a shit,' he muttered, looking in the mirror as he felt the stubble on his chin with a shaking hand. 'Fuck you, an' all,' he said to himself.

Slamming the front door as hard as he'd slammed the cupboard door, he walked off in only a marginal straighter line than he had a few hours ago, back in the direction of the same pub.

There were quite a few people sitting outside on this warm evening and the sound of someone murdering Meatloaf's Bat Out Of Hell coming from inside.

'Karaoke night,' he muttered, with a small grin. He loved karaoke, but Evan would only ever go to them if he couldn't come up with an excuse to be somewhere else.

Don't know why, he was thinking as he drew closer, he knows I love nowt more than a bit of singing.

That should be he knew.

Danny sighed.

Evan never could sing.

At the bar he was served by a waitress with a blue rinse who looked like a walrus on speed. She looked down her large bulbous nose at him. Danny groaned inside. He'd had a few run-ins with her before. The old bat was worse than her miserable flaming son, the bar manager. Not in the mood for any bother with anyone, least of all her, he picked his change up when she slapped it down, said nothing when his pint was shoved over to him, white foam spilling over the top, picked up the wet glass and turned to the stage.

The Meatloaf murderer had been replaced by an attractive middle-aged blonde who really could sing. When she had finished her rendition of Tina Turner's Simply The Best, people stood up and cheered. It was then that Danny caught sight of a couple of old work mates. Carrying his pint aloft, he wound his way through half a dozen tables until he reached them. Pretending not to see the frown on one of their faces, he pulled up a chair and sat down.

'Hi, guys.' He smiled at them, noticing for the first time the two women, who also worked with them. 'Hi Zoë, Elizabeth. What brings you two here, then?'

'Just a night out,' Zoë replied quietly. Zoë was always quiet and most people had to ask her to repeat herself, but tonight she seemed even more so.

'Just a change,' Elizabeth muttered, as she rummaged around in her handbag with her plump fingers, an excuse not to meet his eyes.

Turning to Simon and Todd, he raised his glass. 'Drink up, guys, 'cause you never know when it'll be yer last.'

The one who had frowned at him, Todd- long, lean almost to the point of emaciation, with cheekbones sharp enough to put a knife out of business.' darted a quick glance at Simon.

Simon shrugged, his glasses falling down his nose with the movement.

'What's the matter?' Danny asked.

'Seeing as you're asking, Danny, word is you're bad news to be around. OK?'

'It's not me, it's them.' Danny downed half his pint and put the glass back on the table, before repeating firmly, 'It's them.'

'Who's them?'

'The boss people, them who's in charge.'

The four of them exchanged glances.

'Honest.' Danny nodded sincerely at them.

'What, you mean our bosses at work?' Todd asked.

'No! Them.' Raising his pint to his lips, Danny finished it off. 'Just gonna get another.'

When he had gone, the four of them moved their heads closer. 'How we gonna get rid of him? The daft sod's lost the friggin' plot,' Simon asked.

The girls shook their heads. 'I feel sorry for him,' Elizabeth said.

“Don't,' Todd put in. 'Everyone reckons he's a murderer.'

'So why hasn't he been arrested, then?'

'Probably some stupid technical hitch. You know the law's a load of rubbish these days.'

'But we've worked with him for a few years now. I can't believe he's a murderer.'

'Neither can I, really.' Simon shook his head. 'I actually got on quite well with him.'

'Just saying, that's all,' Todd said.

'Shh, he's back,' Zoë whispered.

Danny sat down. As well as a pint this time, he also had a glass of whiskey. He knocked the whiskey straight back, followed by a large drink of his beer. Wiping his mouth with the back of his hand, he leaned forward and said in a conspiratorial tone, 'It's them.'

'Not again,' Todd said. 'Who the fuck's them?'

'Them. They know everything. How much you have in the bank, how many times you take a shit.'

'Gross.' Elizabeth tutted.

'It's true. Everything is gonna change. The whole world is gonna change. Better be prepared.'

'Where are you getting all this from, Danny?'

'They're watching all the time.' He picked up his pint, swallowed the lot and turned to the couple on the next table. 'They're watching you, an' all.'

The woman frowned at him, and turned away to look at the stage. Her husband did the same. Shrugging, Danny turned back to his work colleagues. 'I'm due back in next Monday. Never thought I would make it a few days ago.'

'Why?' Simon asked, ignoring the nudge from Todd.

'Them.'

'Back to them again, eh?' Todd said sarcastically.

His sarcasm went right over Danny's head. 'They know everything about you. I mean everything.' He waved, his hand enclosing all four of them.

'So you said.' Todd rose. 'Anyone else want a drink?'

'Me please,' 'Zoë smiled.

Elizabeth shook her head. 'None for me, but I'll have a packet of cheese and onion crisps.'

“I'll have a pint, mate.' Danny grinned at Todd.

'I'm not your mate, so get your own in.' Todd weaved his way to the bar, which was proving more and more difficult as the place was now full to the brim.

'What's his problem?' Danny's grin slipped into a frown as he followed Todd with his eyes.

'Don't you think you've had enough, Danny?' Elizabeth said. 'Maybe you should just go home.'

'No,' Danny replied stubbornly. 'Haven't had a sing yet.'

'You're not getting up, are you?' Simon asked.

'Why aye, man. You know I like to sing.'

Todd arrived back at the table with the drinks on a tray. Before he put the tray on the table, Danny snatched the pint meant for Simon. 'Cheers, mate,' he said, before taking a large drink.

Simon shook his head at Todd, mouthing, 'It doesn't matter. Just leave it.'

Gritting his teeth, Todd said, 'That right? You're getting up to sing?'

'Don't I always?'

'It's about time someone told you that you sound like a frog farting up a drainpipe.'

'Who, me?'

'Come on, Todd, he's not that bad.' Simon tried to hide a grin.

'I'm better than him.' Danny pointed at the small sixty year old man who had just left the stage.

'Marginally,' Todd replied.

'I'll show you.' Danny jumped up. He stood still for a moment until the room stopped spinning, then headed for the stage.

'What the hell did you want to wind him up for?' Simon hissed at Todd. 'The poor bugger's going through enough already.'

'Yeah, so you say. I for one think he's guilty as hell.'

Simon sighed. 'Dunno. Just can't believe it.'

At the stage, Danny snatched the mike as it was being handed to someone else, who just shrugged and stepped back. Telling the girl who ran the karaoke the song he wanted, he turned back to face the audience. Suddenly a deathly silence descended over the pub. Clearing his throat, Danny started to sing Make The World Go Away. He hadn't reached the first chorus when the four men who had been in the fish shop the night before, and were now standing at the bar, started to boo him. Soon everyone in the pub was doing the same.

Danny carried on for a few more beats before the tears came. The music was still playing as he collapsed to his knees, and started sobbing his heart out.

Most of the crowd carried on booing, but Elizabeth and

Simon jumped up and helped Danny down from the stage.

With Todd and Zoë's reluctant help they got him outside, but he was inconsolable. Curled in upon himself, his sobs became even louder and his speech, when he managed to say anything between the sobbing, more and more incoherent.

'That lad needs an ambulance,' said the barmaid, who had followed them out. 'Trust me, I've seen this happen before. The lad's had a breakdown.'

CHAPTER FIFTY-SIX

Smiler and Robert were sharing a pepperoni pizza with Louise, who had just finished telling Smiler about her role as the bird woman. Smiler had been amazed to find that at least five of them played the part. They were a brilliant source of information for the sisterhood. The bird woman, whichever one she was, never missed a thing. She knew exactly who came in and out of Scotland Yard.

'But hasn't anyone noticed that there are more than one of you? What if you were on a CCTV camera at the same time?'

'The chances of that are so rare, it's practically impossible, especially as most of them are black and white. Plus, we know where all the cameras are, and take care not to be on them if it can be helped. You have no idea how many times the bird woman has been on the CCTV when they are in the area, and never been noticed.' She smiled at him.

Smiler nodded. It had been good to learn just how extended and organised the sisterhood was, but sad to know that a lot of the safe houses stood empty, sometimes for years.

'So, is the government involved with the Families?'

'Not as such,' Robert replied. 'Certain members, yes. Part of our job at the moment is to gather information on these members.' He put the slice of half-eaten pizza on the plate. 'Really, I shouldn't have had that third piece.'

'Rita's gonna kill you,' Louise laughed.

'She will if that new red dress is too tight,' Robert moaned.

Laughing, Louise stood up. 'I'm going to sit with Lynne for a bit. I believe Robert has something to tell you, Smiler.'

Smiler gave Louise a rueful half smile. He was actually dreading what was to come.

CHAPTER FIFTY-SEVEN

Prince Carl swooped down on the private airport after doing a full circuit, and made a perfect landing on the airstrip. A car was waiting to take him to the house, only a few minutes away. He'd had time to do plenty of thinking on the way over. The sky had been good to him and kept calm right to the end, showing nothing but a clear crystal blue the whole trip. He got into the chauffeur-driven car and, when his luggage had been deposited into the boot, they made their way to the house.

On the steps, he bumped into Billy Slone. Small, thick set and bald, Slone was American, the Family Slone having migrated there from Egypt two hundred years ago. His family specialised in pharmaceuticals.

As they shook hands, Slone said in a quiet voice, 'We need to talk, somewhere private.'

Prince Carl turned to the porter who was standing behind him. 'Put those in my room.' Turning back to Slone, he said, 'Fancy a stroll?'

'Yeah. Why not?' Slone smiled.

Together they went down the steps and, guessing rightly that Slone, a rose lover and grower, would head for the rose garden, Prince Carl fell into step beside him.

'So, how's things?' Slone asked.

'Please, you know I'm not here for your company.'

'Well, if you put it bluntly, neither am I. You are a rather boring piece of work.'

'Thank you.'

Slone burst out laughing. 'Come on, Carl, you know I'm only joking.'

'Are you, though?'

Slone heaved a sigh. 'Look, I've told you I'm on your side. I don't want the peasants culled any more than you do. If they go, who am I going to sell my pills to?' He grinned.

'Look, no more pissing about, Slone. We both know that there are wars going on around the world that have been deliberately started, just to cut the numbers down. Maniacs left in charge of countries because we want them there, no other reason than that, Because it's good for us. But it's time for change. Let them be. What the hell more do we need? Enough bloodshed, I say.'

'Well, that's been done before, remember? How many dead in the last world war? It worked, as well.'

'What!'

'All I'm saying is, Carl, that sometimes it's necessary to cull them. They breed at such an alarming rate. Why can't they all do what China does? One child.'

'Because the west wouldn't go for it. There would be massive uprisings.'

'Now, there's a thought.'

'Please, you've got to help me stop this- this plan.'

'Lighten up, Carl. 'I've already told you that I'm with you. Now chillax, as they say, and look at these gorgeous roses. And the scent.' He stopped walking and sniffed the air. 'And the colours! Have you ever seen anything more beautiful? I love coming here, the garden's a delight… Instead of stressing about the peasants, Carl, take pleasure in what's around you.'

Prince Carl couldn't believe what he was hearing. All those lives at stake, and all this prat was bothered about was a garden full of fucking roses. Am I the only sane one left?

CHAPTER FIFTY-EIGHT

Mike spotted the guy who had been following him for the last hour. He was standing outside the Tesco Express, trying to see in through the window. Mike was watching him over the top of the tins of baked beans. The man turned to look in his direction, and Mike ducked.

Who the----? he wondered. A more scrawny, skinny wreck of a man would be hard to find. He looked like an alkie who had not seen the inside of a shower cubicle for months.

Circling the store, walking out behind the checkout tills while the man looked anywhere but at him, Mike was outside in moments and tapping the man on his shoulder. The man spun round and gaped at Mike, showing brown stumps of uneven teeth. 'You!'

'Yes, me.'

How did you----?'

'It was easy.'

'Oh.'

'Why are you following me?'

'Because I was told to.'

Mike sighed, wondering whether to play rough- 'cause it certainly wouldn't take much to frighten this one-sentence guy- or just carry on being polite, for the sake of anonymity. Choosing the latter, he said, 'So who told you?'

'Rita.'

'Rita!'

The man nodded. 'Yes, Rita.'

'So how long are you supposed to follow me around, and why?'

'Dunno.'

'What do you mean, you don't know? You don't know for how long, or you don't know why?'

'Dunno.'

'Jesus Christ!'

The man shrugged. Staring at Mike, he smiled. Mike was trying really hard not to clench his teeth and yell at him, even though he was driving Mike crazy, when the man said, 'She'll tell me when we get close.'

'So you're just going to follow me around until we get close to Rita?'

He nodded again.

'Why, for fuck's sake?'

'Rita's busy with Smiler.'

'What?'

'Rita's----'

Mike stopped him. 'Yes, I heard.' Mike's emotions were mixed to find that Smiler had disobeyed him and come down to London. 'The little sod,' he muttered.

Honestly, don't know why I'm surprised. Bet he's got the mutt with him an' all.

He looked at the man. 'OK, where do we go from here?'

'Dunno.'

'Don't you know where Rita lives?'

'No, but she'll find me.' He pointed with a nicotine stained finger to his head. 'In here.'

Not another one, Mike thought. Shaking his own head, he turned away and headed up the street. Pulling his cigarettes out, he lit one up and was about to put them away when the man who was dogging his steps said, 'Can I have one of those, please?'

Turning round, Mike handed him a cigarette. For a moment he smiled, knowing that it was usually he who was bumming cigarettes off people. 'Plan on following me forever?' he asked, the smile fading.

'Thank you,' the man said, taking the cigarette and putting it between his lips, before mumbling out the corner of his mouth, 'Only until Rita says she's ready for you.'

'Anything I can do to discourage you?'

The man shook his head, then lit the cigarette up.

'Are we near her?'

'Don't know.' He took a draw off his cigarette.

'So you've got no idea where she lives?'

'No.' He took another draw.

'Fucking hell. You taking the piss or what?'

Again, he shook his head.

'OK.' Mike shrugged and, turning, continued on his way, his stalker still in tow.

They were near the Houses of Parliament when Mike heard a gurgling sound behind him. He turned to see his personal stalker land on his knees and clutch at his throat. Frowning, Mike bent down to help him, but before his outstretched hand could touch the man, he was surrounded on all sides, a black sack pulled quickly down over his head.

Mike tried gamely to fight, but there were too many of them. He felt himself lifted off his feet and carried to his right, where he knew he'd just passed a side street. He tried to yell, but was punched in the side of his head. The next moment he was bundled into a car.

CHAPTER FIFTY-NINE

Smiler was watching the TV, but not really taking in what was on the screen- some wildlife programme about a pride of lions, which actually looked quite tame. Probably out of some zoo, he was thinking, when Rita came into the room. She was wearing a short blue skirt, with a cream top and matching cardigan. Smiler guessed she didn't realise just how much she blended in with the walls. Or, then again, he thought, what do I know?

'I thought you would be more comfortable hearing what I have to say from me,' Rita said.

His heart rate picking up, Smiler gave Rita a brief nod. He was actually dreading what was coming. He'd buried his mother and her evil ways a long time ago, and was not too keen on having her resurrected again.

'OK.' Rita sat down. 'Your mother. I know you've picked up a lot from me, as well as the buzz on the streets. But there's a lot you don't know. You've met the young girl next door.' He motioned with his head to the room.

Smiler nodded, staring at Rita, praying for her to hurry up and get on with it.

'Well, once over, that was your mother.'

'You mean----?'

'Yes. She was once a prisoner of the Families. But not like Lynne, sold, used and abused. No, your mother was in the same place as my mother - an experimental lab.'

'What, like them poor smoking dogs?'

'Not quite, this was…is a laboratory that deals in all things of the mind. That's how you and I, and quite a few others, are the way we are today.'

'You mean, like we inherited it?'

'Yes. Believe me, this was a side effect they never even dreamed of, and are now doing their very best to eradicate. They know that some of us are out here, but even their best can't find us. They first started these experiments in the 30s, between wars, to breed an army that would do everything they were told to do -even turning on their own if needed-and whose legions could be controlled by thought alone. They actually engineered both wars to whittle the population down, and in their paranoia decided they needed their own private army in case the population found out about the Families and turned on them.'

Smiler stared at the floor, his mind in a turmoil. On first thoughts, it seemed a bit far-fetched, but he'd read books about experiments done between and during the wars, even seen pictures that were so horrendous he'd cried in secret, hidden away down some dark alley or at the back of the library where no one ever went. So God only knew what had been hidden from the general public and never made it into print.

'OK, so what about----'

'Your mother.'

Smiler took a deep breath, let it out, and said, 'Yes.'

'She escaped. I don't know how, but she must have been very brave. From what I've been told, she was pregnant with you before they captured her, only no one knew. Least of all your mother.'

'But why did they take her in the first place? Why her, out of all the other fucking girls she must have known? Any particular reason, or was she just randomly picked off the street?'

At that moment, things began to change for Smiler. His mother, who he had hated for as long as he could remember, had been as much a pawn in all of this as he was.

'Because,' Rita answered, 'she was one of the special ones. As a child, she must have shown very high cognitive powers without even knowing it. A conversation overheard, a form filled in. A teacher's report in her early years. Because once upon a time, our sixth sense was stronger than it is now, much stronger. The Families decided to weed it out centuries ago. And trust me, their spies are everywhere. Anyhow, she did manage to escape, and was found by one of the sisterhood. You were born in the room that Lynne is in now.'

Smiler gulped. He looked around with fresh eyes, before saying, 'So, how did she end up on the streets?'

'I was only about twelve at the time, my own mother had escaped years before, there were eleven escapees in that decade.'

'Eleven in ten years!

'And that was a good total. Anyhow from what I'm told, your mother just disappeared off the radar. They tried to find her, but she was clever, your mother. I'm told that the reason she took to drink and drugs was to mask it all out. She knew that the sisterhood were against such things, but she couldn't stand it any more. The constant buzz in her head was driving her crazy.'

'So she took me to hell instead.'

Rita sighed. 'They tried to find her, Smiler.'

Smiler jumped up. Pushing his chair over, he shouted, 'Look at me! Look at my face! They didn't fucking try hard enough.' He started walking back and forth, his body trembling. Suddenly he stopped, and faced Rita. 'Look at this.' He pulled his sleeve up, exposing slash mark after slash mark, a whole train track of scars. Unrolling that sleeve, he pulled up the other one, where the lines were repeated. 'Look at me. Take a good look, you fucking bastard.'

Sensing his distress, Tiny whined and nudged him with his nose, but Smiler ignored him. Rita had been prepared for this outburst. Calmly, she stood and said, 'They did try, Smiler, but drink and drugs mask any signals coming from the mind. Your mother knew this, and it's what she chose to do. Probably the only thing she could do.'

Smiler sat back down. Tiny, staring up at Smiler's face, got as close as he could and rested his head on Smiler's knee.

'So,' Smiler said after a minute, staring at the top of the dog's head. 'Where's your mother? Bet she didn't treat you the way mine treated me.'

Rita knew that the presence of the dog had a calming effect on Smiler. It had worked before with others. The safe houses scattered around the country had been home to many cats and dogs.

'She's with them,' she said quietly.

'What!'

Rita nodded. 'She was recaptured when I was seven. The sisterhood brought me up----'

Suddenly Rita stopped talking. Smiler, who had been about to say something, stared at her. He knew why her face showed shock. He had felt the emptiness at the same moment.

'Mike's gone. He…he's nowhere.'

Rita muttered. 'Nowhere Man.'

'Is he dead?'

Rita shook her head. 'I don't know.'

CHAPTER SIXTY

Aunt May put the phone down as Brother David came in from the garden. He was carrying a basket full of freshly picked carrots. 'Good crop this year, Aunt May.' He smiled. 'So, now you've had your nap, are you going to tell me more?'

'OK, bloody well sit down then, or I'll have a stiff neck in the morning from staring up at you.'

Brother David took the basket into the kitchen and returned with a glass of water. Placing it within reach on the coffee table, he sat down and looked expectantly at Aunt May.

'You know quite a bit about the Families, but trust me- it's not them you have to fear, so much as their agents.'

'Agents?'

'Yup. These are the ones who really hold the reins. The Families make the decisions, or think they do. But the basic day to day running is left to the agents, who sometimes just tell the Families what they want to hear.'

'So it's wheels within wheels.'

'Oh, yes.'

'Right then, dear. I wish you would stop going round in circles and tell me exactly what it is we're facing here.'

'Death.'

'What?'

'Yes, which is why you have to lose the bloody sackcloth and get some ordinary clothes. As soon as you step off the island, maybe even while you're on it, you'll be recognised at once. There's a bloody price on your head.'

Brother David's face paled to an off-white colour. 'When were you going to tell me?'

'About two minutes ago, as soon as I got the bloody phone call, OK? So move it. We've got to get off the island tonight.'

'But the tide's in for most of the night. How are we going to manage it with the causeway under water?'

'Don't fret, it's sorted.' Aunt May had got out of her seat and was heading for the stairs when they both heard a loud knocking on the door.

Aunt May looked quickly at Brother David. Putting her finger to her lips, she whispered, 'Upstairs. I'll sort this.' Brother David nodded.

Aunt May moved to the door. But the handle was already turning.

CHAPTER SIXTY-ONE

The meeting was set to take place in the large ballroom of the hotel. Half of the hall was taken up with seats, facing a stage hung with velvet curtains of the same blood-red as the carpet. The chandeliers matched the ones that graced the hall, and the other half of the room had pine flooring for dancing and greeting, and a large buffet table at the end of the room filled with food from every corner of the globe.

Worldwide, the major players of the Families numbered twenty-five. Below them were the agents, the people who did most of the work and earned themselves a very good living. These were mostly cousins, a lot of them many times removed, but Family enough to be totally loyal. Or so the inner circle thought.

This was only the seventh time in history that an extraordinary meeting had been called. Usually, the big meet-up was once a year, and half the time most Family members never turned up, preferring to leave everything to the agents while they indulged in their various lifestyles.

Tony stood next to Kirill Tarasov and Earl James Simmonds.

Tarasov was gritting his teeth, trying to be polite to Simmons, and was pleased to make his excuses to leave when he spotted his daughter Lovilla enter the room. He frowned when he noticed who she was with.

Walking up to her, talking politely on the way to people, most of whom he couldn't bear the sight of, he calmed himself by taking a few deep breaths before reaching her.

'Hello Lovilla.' Leaning forward, he kissed her cheek.

'Hello, Father.' She smiled up at him before kissing him back.

Straightening up, Tarasov nodded at Count Rene. 'Hello, Rene. Good trip over?'

'Quality, Kirill, quality.' He looked Tarasov in the eye. 'Would either of you like a drink?' he asked politely, knowing that Tarasov would rather choke to death than drink with him.

'No, thank you, I have someone to see.'

Count Rene nodded at him.

'Coming, Lovilla?' Tarasov asked, eyebrow raised.

Her smile was full of arrogance as she declined, and slipped her arm through Count Rene's.

Tarasov was foaming as he turned and strode towards the bar. But he knew better than to let it show. So that's the game you're playing, is it, daughter? he thought.

'Hmm.' He smiled despite his anger, although he was thinking, Coming out to play with the grownups, eh?

'Vodka,' he snapped at Ella, who had been transferred from

her cleaning duties to serve behind the bar.

Ella handed over the vodka. She knew all about Tarasov and his vile habits. She'd spent two weeks at his villa, before she'd been taken to Africa to spend a further year in a foul, stinking, diseased brothel. An American soldier, who was a frequent visitor, had been responsible for freeing her. He had helped her to escape one night, equipped with decent clothes and enough money for a passage to England. There, having heard rumours about them, she had sought out the sisterhood.

Knowing so many girls passed through his hands that he probably had no chance of remembering her, and seeing as the supervisor was watching, she smiled at Tarasov, who completely ignored her.

Lifting the glass to his mouth, Tarasov couldn't help but wonder why his illegal son, born of a peasant, had turned out to be a much better man than his legal wimp of a son- who still hadn't turned up. 'Typical,' he muttered, putting the glass back on the bar. 'Just when I need the prat.'

Spotting the American, Slone, Tarasov downed his drink and walked over to him. The American's greeting was friendly enough, even though he had to look up at Tarasov. 'Hi Tarasov. Bet it's nice to be back in the warmth again.'

'Actually, the cold suits my blood temperature.'

Slone grinned. 'I just bet it does. You ready to do battle in the morning?'

'Oh yes.'

Tarasov surveyed the room, weighing up those for and those against, wondering if he could rely on any of them. And when his damn son was going to turn up, if ever.

Spotting Prince Carl, he was about to go and see him when Tony came over and whispered in his ear.

Quickly Tarasov glanced at his watch. The meeting was scheduled for nine o' clock in the morning. It was tradition, family only. Midday, another meeting would be held and the agents would be told what they needed to be told. Tonight was for socialising, getting the right people on board.

Precious time that he needed.

'Damn,' he muttered. Probably just over an hour to London, perhaps more. But he had to go. He nodded at Tony, then caught the eye of his three bodyguards and gestured with his head for them to meet him outside.

CHAPTER SIXTY-TWO

Danny woke up, wondering where he was. His vision was blurred and he couldn't move his hands. He blinked a few times, and suddenly two faces swam above his head.

They were close and peering down at him. Their mouths were moving, but he couldn't hear what they were saying. One of them leaned further over. It was then, moving his head slightly in the direction of that face, that he saw the bars on the window. He tried to scream, but nothing came out. His mouth was full of cotton wool. Panicking, he started to thrash about, then each of them grabbed an arm and hoisted him up. One kept hold of him while the other filled a syringe with white liquid.

He tried to free his arms, but it was hopeless. It was then he realised he was in a straitjacket.

'Help!' he screamed, over and over, unaware that hardly any sound was coming out. Wild-eyed, he watched as the one with the syringe stuck it into his arm.

Who are they?

Where am I?

It's them.

Oh my God, it's them.

He pleaded with his eyes. But they said nothing, just stared at him.

A few moments later, he was floating on air. Then his head fell to one side, and Danny slowly closed his eyes.

CHAPTER SIXTY-THREE

'Hi, May,' Jill said, as she walked in.

'Hi yourself,' Aunt May answered. She looked at her watch. 'What brings you out in the bloody dark…Thought you had a bad stomach?'

'It's eased off a bit, well quite a lot thank God. Anyhow I thought you might like a bit of company, you know. Bit of gossip. You, by the way, are the topic of the village. The usual shopkeeper's back, and going crazy about what happened. Wouldn't like to be the owners of that agency when he gets his hands on them.' She shrugged her shoulders. 'The girls are up in their bedrooms, probably Facebooking as usual. The TV is crap. Don't know why we pay a licence. I was feeling a bit lonely.'

'You know you're welcome any time. Cup of tea?'

'I'll make it.'

'No.' Aunt May hurried past her into the kitchen. No way was she giving Jill a chance to drop something into her tea. 'Do you want tea or coffee?' Aunt May asked over her shoulder.

'Tea, thanks, coffee keeps me awake if I drink it at night. It's the last thing I need.'

Upstairs, Brother David was looking in the full-length mirror. Mike's jeans were a bit tight around the waist, but bearable, and the black t-shirt fitted all right. It felt strange to be in clothes again. He realised that he'd missed the freedom of movement, without even knowing it.

He'd heard Jill come in, and was reluctant to go downstairs in case she started asking questions. She was bound to wonder why he wasn't wearing his robe. But she will be wondering where I am. Best show my face.

'Hi, Jill,' he said a moment later, as he walked into the kitchen.

Jill blinked. 'My, look at you.'

'Yes, well…'

'His robe needed a wash, so he borrowed some of Mike's clothes,' Aunt May put in quickly, knowing Brother David would struggle to come up with a bare-faced lie.

Brother David smiled at Jill as he nodded in agreement, then quickly turned away, knowing his face was probably red.

'Erm...any word from Mike?' Jill asked.

'No,' Aunt May replied. 'He's probably busy.' She could feel the tension coming from Jill. Brother David was far from a good actor, and truth be told, neither was Jill. The problem was getting her out of the house without raising her suspicions.

She yawned. 'Oh, sorry, Jill.' She laughed.

Jill smiled. 'You're bound to be tired. I'll drink this and go. Perhaps I'll have an early night as well.'

Ten minutes later, Brother David was closing the door behind Jill. 'I thought she was never going to go,' he said.

'Yes, and I've yawned so much I think I've dislocated my bloody jaw.' Aunt May moved her jaw back and forth.

'So what now?'

'Now we go.' Quickly, she picked up her handbag, and got her coat and one of Mike's denim jackets off the pegs by the door.

'Where are we going?' Brother David asked, shrugging into Mike's jacket.

'Norfolk.'

'Norfolk! That's where St Godric was born, in 1065. He actually came to Lindisfarne, and was inspired by St Cuthbert to become a hermit. He…he lived until he was one hundred and ten.'

'Really? If I didn't know any better, I'd think it was bloody Smiler standing there spouting off. Come on.'

Still amazed by the connection, Brother David followed Aunt May out of the house and down to the dock. The speedboat was waiting for them. Patrick, whose boat it was, welcomed them on board and, without wasting any more time, whisked them off down the coast to the small fishing village of Seahouses, where a car was waiting for them.

CHAPTER SIXTY-FOUR

Mike, hands tied behind his back, was also tied to a chair in what looked like a metal-walled room. The black sack had been taken off his head half an hour ago, and replaced by a gag that was driving him crazy. There was one dim light above his head. It was impossible to see into the far corners of the room.

He knew there were three of them. One, who he presumed to be in charge, was sitting at a desk, every now and then throwing a dirty look his way. He was tall and thick set, with a slight Russian accent. The other two, standing at each side of him, were obviously heavies and wouldn't look out of place standing outside of a notorious nightclub.

He struggled with the ropes tying his hands, and received a slap to the side of his head for his efforts. The man at the desk looked up from the papers he'd been going through. Turning the last page over, he laid it on top of the others and glared at Mike.

Just by his face, Mike knew he was in deep shit. Wondering just what the hell he'd ever done to this man, who he'd never seen in his life, he felt the skin crawl on the back of his neck as the man rose from his chair. Not once did he take his eyes off Mike as he walked over and stood in front of him.

The blow came without warning, without a word spoken. One minute he was staring at Mike, the next he was viciously attacking him. Punch after punch rained down on him, from his head to his stomach. Swinging to one side to avoid him, Mike toppled over the chair. Both he and it ended on the floor, where the man proceeded to kick him.

Mike struggled the best he could, but he was helpless and guessed that this was finally it. He wouldn't see this night out. Regrets flashed through his mind, for a moment masking the pain.

Then suddenly he was hauled upright, and his tormentor, who had not said a word throughout the ordeal, was pulled to one side by a bigger man.

'Why?' the newcomer asked.

'So you know who he is then, Father?'

Kirill Tarasov glared at his son.

For a moment, what they were saying went over Mike's head. He was busy looking at the three men standing behind Tarasov.

They could be triplets, he thought. Then he blinked. More than triplets - they're the spitting doubles of these two twats behind me. A strange feeling went through him, and he shuddered.

He tuned back in, just in time to hear the man who had captured him yelling at the newcomer.

'It's always been him, hasn't it? Whatever I did was never

enough, never good enough for you.'

'Nonsense, Vadim,' Tarasov snapped.

'Is it? Ask Lovilla, she'll tell you. We know you've watched him since he was fucking well conceived.'

'OK! Enough. We have to get back to Norfolk.' He looked at the two men standing behind Mike. 'Release him, and take him back to Norfolk. He needs a Family doctor now.'

'Not before he learns the truth.' Vadim stepped in front of Mike. 'Let me introduce you. Detective Inspector Michael Yorke, meet your father - the esteemed Kirill Tarasov.'

What follows next is a short story from the Seahills, to introduce readers who have only read the Mike Yorke books to the Seahills cast. But somehow, a well-known character from the Mike Yorke books has found his way to the Seahills!

HUNGRY EYES

The archaeologist, a tall very thin man with a heavily grey speckled moustache smiled at his audience.

The hall was full of people who had been eager to learn about the recent dig at St Michael and All Angels church in Houghton le Spring. A new floor was being laid, and so the archaeologists had moved in.

His lecture was finished and in summing up, he said, "So what have we learned? That this was once a Prehistoric Ritual site- Perhaps…A Roman Temple? Possibly, it was after all standard practice for Romans to take over earlier religious sites. There is definite evidence of Normans and Saxons, and during the last excavation in the churchyard in the late nineties an erratic line of whinstone boulders, probably from the Hadrian's wall area, do suggest a prehistoric use of the site, several other such boulders have now been found inside the church, so there is a suggestion not proof mind you, but perhaps there was a stone circle on the site."

PC Steven Carter of the ginger hair and countless freckles,

gasped in awe. He couldn't wait to get back to the station and tell his boss, D I Lorraine Hunt. She was always so interested in the history of Houghton le Spring, he thought, as he applauded along with every one else.

As Carter made his way outside, he was followed by three men. The men were locals from the Seahills estate in Houghton le Spring; Carter hadn't noticed them because they had been sitting at the back.

“So what do yer reckon?” Danny Jorden asked his two friends. Danny was a chancer, had been all his life, skirting the boundary between legal and illegal, nothing big-nothing bad, just enough to keep his kids in shoe leather and food on the table.

“Hmm, don't really know.” His cousin Len Jorden scratched his chin, looking sideways at the other member of the trio. Like his cousin, Len was dark- haired with brilliant green eyes, the resemblance ended there though, Danny was tall, thick set and frequently wore a smile, where Len was as tall but even thinner than the archaeologist, plus he permanently had the look of a professional pall bearer.

“You're a bloody old woman Len.” Adam Glazier who at twenty-six was the youngest by nine years, said grinning at Len.

“And your jokes stink” Len retorted

“Knock knock.” Adam laughed.

“Piss off.”

“Shut up the pair of you. What we gonna do, I reckon there's a fortune in coins lying in this old church, we need to get to them before those archaeologist blokes do, and it has to be tonight. Tomorrow they start filling the floor in.”

“It's a damn shame they couldn't go deeper- God knows what they might have found, I mean all those old bones.” Len shivered.

Danny shook his head “That's the point Len, they cant dig any further. but we can.”

“ I don't know, the church in the middle of the night… Kinda spooky if yer ask me.”

“Old woman.” Adam hissed.

“Alright for Gods sake.' Danny snapped, the pressure of new shoes for his oldest making him edgy, “Are youse in or not?”

Adam shrugged, “Yeah fine by me.”

“Len?” Danny turned to his cousin.

Len thought about it for a moment, sighed then answered. “I suppose so. But the first sign of a ghost…”

Adam burst out laughing. “Bloody ghosts, no such thing yer soft shite…We gonna cut Jacko in?”

“Jacko.” Danny thought for a minute. Jacko was a good mate and probably would have been here if he wasn't ill. “Depends what we find I suppose.”

They continued arguing on the way to Danny's van. When they got there Danny kissed his fingers and patted the wing mirror, Len tutted but Danny ignored him. The van, which he called

Elizabeth after his dream woman Elizabeth Taylor, was his pride and joy. At the moment his girl
friend was not speaking to him because three nights ago he'd called out, 'Oh more Elizabeth more,' at totally the wrong moment, and not for the first time either.

As they drove away, another man came out of the church. A tall motley skinned man with a heavy beard, he was talking on his mobile phone in an east European accent, and he was angry. “You get to him and you get to him now, you have two hours or it's your skin I'll be stretching over my lampshade.” He snapped his phone shut and strode over to the waiting Mercedes.

DI Lorraine Hunt glared at her partner Detective Luke Daniels. “I swear I will kill him,” she mouthed, “Any minute now.”

Luke, tall handsome and black, with a presence about him that turned heads, tried not to laugh out loud, as unaware that his boss was reaching melt down, Carter droned on and on about the history of St Michaels and All Angels church.

Two minutes later Lorraine had had enough, she stood up, “ Yeah OK Carter, that's all very interesting, but old bones and stones that may or may
not be four thousand years old can't very well help us with today's problems, can they? ”

Luke smiled, Carter actually got away with more than any-

one in the station, Luke new that Lorraine genuinely liked the young naive officer, who had got it into his head that Lorraine shared his love of the area's
history. But at the moment Luke was as concerned as Lorraine about the news that had come over the wires less than an hour ago.

"So what's up?" Carter asked.

"Fill him in Luke, I'm in need of some liquid refreshment, back in a mo." She left them, her long blonde pony tail swishing from side to side as she strode out of the office.

Five minutes later she was back, a can of diet coke in her hand and seeing the look of horror on Carter's face she guessed Luke had told him most of what there was to know about Kirill Tarasov.

"So." She sat down at her desk, her eyebrows raised in a question.

Carter swallowed hard, then felt sick. "A… a cannibal?"

"Yes. A cannibal that collects antiques."

"There's no accounting for tastes, is there?" Luke said, shaking his head.

Carter and Lorraine groaned in unison, and Lorraine went on "He's been wanted all over the world for years, nearly been caught twice. Believe me this guy makes Dracula look like a pussy cat. He skins his victims, eats them, then decorates his house with their skin."

"Oh gross." Carter shivered. "But why haven't I heard about

him before now?"

"Classified information, there's enough fear in the world today without adding to it, and why give him glory 'cos there's plenty weirdoes out there that would worship him...Actually Kirill, if that's even his real name, if he's even really Russian, is a variant of old Greek which means Lord."

"Yeah, in his case Lord of Darkness. " Luke put in, "And no one's safe when this guys around."

"Please don't tell me he's in Houghton, please." Carter was thinking of his mother, all alone until he got in from work, and it was getting dark out there already. The hairs stood out on the back of his neck, when he thought of the sickly gruesome things Luke had told him.

"Get a grip Carter,' Lorraine said. 'He was followed from Germany to France, where they lost him for the second time this year. But then luck struck and he was recognised getting off a plane in Newcastle. He was followed, but the agent's car died on him. Tarasov was last seen heading for Durham."

Just as Carter opened his mouth to ask more questions the phone rang. Lorraine quickly snatched it up.

The two officers watched her face go from dismay to outright disbelief. She muttered a few words back, put the phone down and stared at Luke and Carter.

"Well?" Luke urged.

Lorraine slowly shook her head, blew air out of her cheeks

before saying, “There's been a prison break at Durham, one man dead, two escapees…Both escapees were doing life for murder…Vicious murder.” she stood up, “Come on guys, we're all out on patrol.”

It was a dark night, no stars and hardly any moon, Danny, Len and Adam met up outside of the church. They had each taken different routes up from the Seahills; knowing that some of the gossips on the estate hardly slept, and if the three of them were seen together after midnight, two and two would have been put together and come out with an odd number.

“So where we gonna dig first?” Len whispered.

“I reckon up the front near the altar.” Danny replied.

Adam nodded. “Sounds good to me.”

Quietly they made their way to the door, Danny pulled out a crowbar and set to work on the heavy locks. “Once upon a time Church's used to be open at all times,” he grunted as he struggled with the lock.

“Aye, but that was before thieving bastards started to rob them.” Adam said with conviction.

Len looked at him, “So what the hell are we then?”

Adam shrugged, “That's different. We're not exactly robbing the church. I reckon coins and ancient stuff belong to the people, it's our…Our birthright.” he nodded at Len then at Danny.

“Will the pair of yers shut the fuck up and give me a hand for

Christ's sake."

"OK, OK, keep yer hair on." Adam lent his weight to Danny's and the lock snapped with a sudden loud sound reminiscent of a gunshot.

"Shit." Len ducked and quickly looked around.

Slowly as they all held their breaths, Danny pushed the door open, expecting it to start creaking at any moment. But the hinges were well oiled and the door opened silently. "Remember," he hissed, "Keep the torches pointed at the ground; we don't want any lights showing through the windows."

They crept along to the altar, they were three feet away from their target when Len squealed.

"What the…?" Danny glared at him.

"Yer nearly frightened the life outta me, yer git prat." Adam gave Len a push.

"Something ran over me foot." Len muttered.

"I'll run over yer fucking foot in a minute, here." Danny thrust a spade at Len. "This is as good a place as any."

"It was probably a rat." Adam whispered. "Or," he grinned, "Maybes a ghost."

Len glared at him as he started digging. Danny pulled a lantern and another spade out of the holdall. He handed the spade to Adam then lit the lantern. The light spread over a six foot radius, enough for them to see what they were doing. All three of them started digging in a yard- wide square.

Twenty minutes later Len's spade hit something solid.

"Oh my God." He dropped to his knees quickly followed by the others. With Adam holding the torches, Len and Danny began to scrape away at the soil. In moments they uncovered a large metal box.

"That doesn't look really old." Len observed, though he had to keep his feet solid on the ground to stop from dancing with excitement. He sighed deeply and the others knew how he felt. Rich at last. Was the one thought that was running through their heads.

"It's bloody heavy though." Groaning Danny lifted the box and carried it to the Alter.

Practically slavering, Adam rubbed his hands together with excitement,

"Bet it's full of gold coins. We should have had Jacko here."

"He could hardly get out of bed this morning with the flu." Len stared at the box as Danny stepped back. "But we'll see he's alright won't we Danny?"

Kirill Tarasov watched as the two he'd been waiting for ran from behind the trees to the car, he noticed one of them limping badly and frowned; a weakling. When they had climbed into the back of the Mercedes he turned towards them.

"Everything went to plan then?" He eyed them up and instantly dismissing the smaller man who had limped and was less than skin and bone. To register on Tarasovs radar you needed some meat on your bones.

"Yeah." Simon Dupri, alias the Slasher, a nickname he'd been given by the press, answered quickly. " He definitley buried the box in the church, in front of the alter. He swore this as the bastard begged for his life."

The smaller man, Vinnie Grey sniggered, he was doing life for murdering his whole family, then starting on his neighbours one dark winter night. He was cut short by a look from Tarasov.

"OK." Tarasov pulled into the road, "We go to the church now, and you tell me all about how he died on the way."

And you skinny man, he thought, will not be coming out of the church. Fatso though, I will keep close in case rations are hard to come by someday
soon.

"Open it, open it." Adam practically shouted.

"Shh." Danny and Len hissed.

For a moment there was silence, Adam took a deep breath and controlled himself before nodding at the other two. Slowly Danny pried the lid off the box, then gasped when he heard a sound behind him. Quickly the three of them spun round.

There was nothing but the pitch darkness with a lighter patch right it the back where the stained glass window in all its glory reigned supreme. Len wiped the sweat off his brow, as Adam placed a shaking hand over his heart.

"Just the fucking rats again." Danny snapped, turning back to the box.

The lid was off now and all three holding their breath in anticipation peered inside.

Tarasov, followed by Dupri and Grey, quietly made their way past the old gravestones to the church When they reached the door, Tarasov held his hand up to stop the others as he stared in dismay at the broken lock.

He clenched his fists as he gritted his teeth. He had searched for years for the box. He would not be out done now. Quickly he put his finger to his lips, quelling any outbursts from the others, as he cocked his head like an inquisitive dog listening, stretching his senses.

At first he heard nothing, he stepped through the door and paused, listening again concentrating hard, turning his head he looked towards the alter, his eyes adjusted to the darkness saw the light beneath the alter beckoning like a beacon.

Bastards!

"Hurry up, hurry up." Adam unable to control himself any longer, urged. "What is it…Is it gold coins? Fucking just tell us man."

Just as exited, Len on the other side squashed up to his cousin, "What's in…Are we rich? Bloody hell I can't stand this any more- how much?"

Frowning Danny pulled a large piece of carefully folded canvas out of the box. He held it up while the others shone their torches. “Oh for God's sake, it's just a bloody painting.” Unable to hide his disappointment, he shook his head. “It's a painting of a woman, who believe me is no Elizabeth Taylor.”

“Yer can say that again.” Adam stared at the painting. “I've seen that ugly mug some where before though.”

Len tutted, “Oh you bloody pair of idiots, for God's sake it's the Mona Lisa.”

Danny and Adam stared at Len, after a moment Danny said. “Do yer think it's the real I am?”

Len looked in awe at the signature. Slowly he nodded.

“Is it worth anything?” Adam beat Danny to the question.

The answer came from behind them. “Yes gentlemen…millions.”

For a moment they froze, then slowly as if trained by a choreographer, they turned together. Danny swallowed hard, he could feel Adam and Len trembling at his sides- and who could blame them, faced with this huge man who held a large knife in each hand.

Tarasov moved closer. “For years I have followed this painting, then seven years ago the trail went cold. The fools in the museum think they have the real one. Ha.”

“What er, what yer gonna do like?” Danny asked, trying really hard but not quite succeeding to keep the tremble out of his voice, though judging by the mans face he could well guess just what he was going to do.

He smiled at them and Len trembled even more. Adam though found his voice. “Who are you like? Standing there like some crazy fuck out of a horror movie. Think we're frightened like?”

“You should be, cocky twat.” Grey said, stepping out from behind Tarasov.

“Oh God.” Len moaned. “We're well and truly up shit creek without a paddle this time guys.” A second later he screamed as he was grabbed from behind.

Lens scream forced Adam into action. Without thinking he threw himself at Grey, leaving Danny to deal with Tarasov and his knives. Len bent over then quickly threw his head back, snapping his assailants nose. More by luck than anything else, Adam kicked Grey in the exact spot on his injured leg, when he yelled in pain and reached for his leg; Adam launched a left hook and knocked him out flat.

As Len was peeling himself from the dead weight that was still clinging onto him, Adam quickly moved to Danny's side.

Tarasov laughed, “You think you can take me? Ha I don't think so. Not even two or three of you.” He jumped forward and the knife in his right hand slashed down taking a piece of Adam's ear off and slicing the side of his neck. Blood spurted as Adam collapsed to his knees in shock.

Advancing on Danny, Tarasov laughed again.

"Fuck off." Danny yelled. Wondering if this would be a good time to run, but knowing he couldn't leave Adam at the mercy of this grinning freak.

Then he had a brain wave, quickly he snatched the painting up, he shook the canvas and Tarasov stopped, a look of pure horror on his face.

"No, no…Do not damage it. Do not damage it." His eyes burned into Danny's. "I will give you anything."

"Do yer honestly think for one minute that I'd trust you, yer creepy bastard." Danny shook the painting again, as Len finally untangled from Dupri bent down to help Adam.

Tarasov curled his lip, "Enough of this," he shouted, his arms held high. Each long blade caught the light as he prepared to leap forward again.

"Oh yes well said, definitely enough of this." DI Lorraine Hunt said as she, Luke Daniels and Carter hurried into the church.

They had been cruising round the Seahills estate, visiting a couple of known criminals who had recently been released from Durham prison when Lorraine had suddenly remembered something Carter had said about the church, on a hunch they had quickly sped up to Houghton. "Kirill Tarasov I am arresting you on…Well, just about any crime known to man."

"Fucking hell." Danny wiped sweat from his brow. "Talk about saved by the bell." He bent down to see to Adam, but Len was staring at him and shaking his head.

"NO." Danny yelled.

Using the sudden distraction Tarasov ran at Lorraine, but she was ready for him. Quickly she moved to the side and as Tarasov ran past her she kicked his leg from underneath him. He fell to the floor and Carter and Luke were on top of him in seconds.

Luke cuffed him. Tarasov looked at Lorraine; mixed with the contempt there was a smattering of admiration as he said. "Brought down by a woman!"

"Save it creep." Lorraine answered moving to Adam. Quickly she felt for a pulse, it took her a minute but she found it, very erratic but still a pulse, taking Len's hand she pressed it over the wound in Adams neck. "Keep it there…Carter." She looked over her shoulder, "Ambulance."

"On its way boss."

Danny and Len breathed twin sighs of relief. Lorraine looked at them, shook her head, and said, "Please tell me why I am not at all surprised to find you lot here."

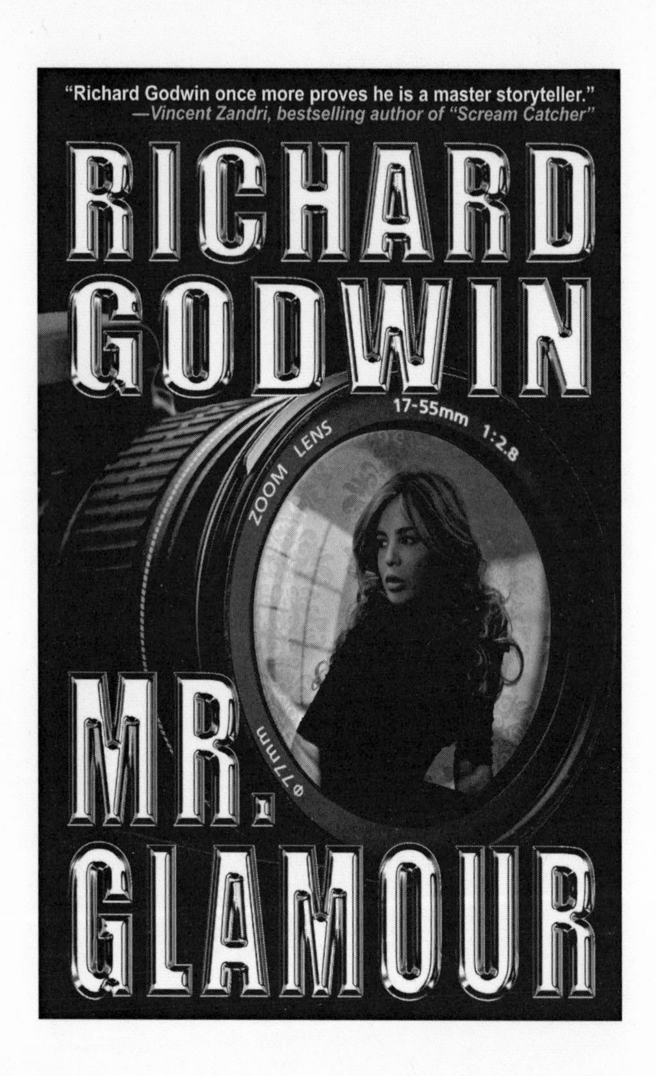
"Richard Godwin once more proves he is a master storyteller."
—Vincent Zandri, bestselling author of "Scream Catcher"
RICHARD
GODWIN
17-55mm 1:2.8
ZOOM LENS
ø77mm
MR.
GLAMOUR